# Snatched
# Away
## Her Innocence Was Stolen

Alexis D. Smith-Jones

Credits

Cover designed by Designed Creativity, LLC.

ISBN:1976069904
ISBN-13:9781976069901

# DEDICATION

This book is dedicated to my kids, Travis Jr., Samar, King, Nelani, and Tyrane. I want you to always go after what you want. Never let anyone tell you it isn't possible. Work hard for whatever you want and never give up. Know that your momma is always going to be your biggest fan and will still have your back to push you in the right direction to fulfill the great destiny that has already been set out for you. Thank you all for being my motivation and my reason to keep pushing. Always remember don't ever let someone who gave up on their dreams talk you out of yours.

Love Always and Forever, Ma.

# CONTENTS

# ACKNOWLEDGMENTS

First, I would like to thank God for allowing me the ability to share my gift of writing finally. I would like to thank my husband, Travis Jones. Thank you for always pushing me to go for what I want and believing in me when I didn't believe in myself, and for still being a team player. Your support and love I am forever grateful. My mother, Eleanor Butler, and my father, Waidus Smith for bringing me into this world and for always loving me. ALL my sisters, those that are related by blood and those by soul, thank you all for being my first friends. My Gelatis (you ladies know who you are), thank you for always being there for me. Nandi Patterson, Feiona Dupree, Stephanie Foster, and Ebony Wilson, love you so much, thank you for always being there to support me no matter what it is, and you will forever hold a special place in my heart no matter where life may take us. My cousin, Katrina Edwards, thank you for always bringing such positivity into my life. My brother Arthur (LA) Walker, I love you so much. To those who I may have forgotten to mention by name just know that you hold a special place in my heart. To everyone who supports me thank you all so much. I love you all forever.

Love Always,
Lexis

# *START OF IT ALL*

The sunshine state was never good to me. I'm Mia Johnson and was born in Miami, Florida. I was my mom and dad's only child together. Born into a dysfunctional family is what I've heard a lot of people say. My mom was left in the hospital when she was a baby and was raised by what most would called an angel from above. She never knew who her dad was, but we believe he's white or Spanish. She had a daughter before me right out of high school and then she had me seven years later. Although my parents were never married, they were in love and ready to build a life together, at least that's what I was made to believe. I completed their dream of one big happy family, and there was no doubt that my parents Lisa and Andre loved me.

My parents happily ever after was short-lived, and they never made it to marriage. When I was only four years old, my mom decided that she could no longer deal with my dad's cheating and him not being able to commit to her or their relationship. "Andre how could you just pick up and leave and not even tell me." My mother screams through the phone at my dad. "After all that you've put me through, you just up and leave because you think you've found someone better and think she can take care of you." My mom threw the phone. The summer before my 5th birthday my dad moved out with his new woman. Leaving me, my mom, and my big sister, Rachel without even letting us know he was gone. It didn't really bother me much at first because every weekend since he moved out my dad was there to pick me up. I always had something to look forward to at the end of the week. I couldn't wait for Friday to come. No matter what my mom and dad went through, daddy made sure that I knew he loved and cherished me. Not long after my dad was with Tamara, they ended up married, and I now had a step-mother.

Every Monday when I would come back from with my dad I would tell my mom all about the exciting things I did with him and his new wife, Tamara. "Mommy we went swimming, and daddy took Tamara and me out to dinner and the movies. And they let me pick the movie," I ran into the house excited. While rolling her eyes, she always responded the same way, "Oh, he still with her? He's only with her for her money." I just didn't understand why my mom wasn't happy that I was. I guess my mom was holding on to the hopes of having her dreamed family with my dad even though he had done her wrong so many times when they were together. Andre went as far as having another baby with another woman while they were together. The more I came home telling her about my weekend with my dad and his new wife the more it destroyed her dream of having her family back together.

After my mom and dad broke up she never fully got over my dad. I mean she had a couple of friends for a little while, and then we wouldn't see them anymore. "Momma what happen to your friend Chris," Rachel asked while we were riding in the car. "Oh child, I don't have time for him." That was usually her answer every time one of her friends would no longer come around. I think my mom was running them off just in case my dad ever decided he wanted to come back. It went on like that for about two years.

That is until mom finally meets someone that may take her mind off Andre. Two years after they split and a couple of friends later while mom, Rachel and I were doing a little shopping. After shopping, as we walked to the car a handsome man pulled up in a beautiful, clean gold convertible Jaguar. "Excuse me Ms., but I was wondering if I could have a minute or two of your time?" Rachel took me and we got in the car while mom stopped, and the man walked over to meet her where she was standing. "Rachel who is that man and what is that piece of paper he is giving momma?" I asked as I was looking out the window. "Mia sit down, and I don't know that man or what he is giving momma on that paper girl, it's probably his phone number," Rachel responded as she also was looking out the window.

Three or four months had passed since mom had met the man in the nice car. I saw him a couple of times picking my mom up and dropping her off, but I had never spent any time with him. As far as I knew he was just my mom's friend. One Friday while I was waiting for my dad who was running late the doorbell rings. Rachel goes to open the door, and I was standing right beside her expecting to see my dad, instead it was my mom's friend with the nice car. "Hey momma your friend is here, and he got some funny looking boys...." Rachel quickly covers my mouth she did that a lot. She always said I didn't care what I let come out my mouth and I was too outspoken. Rachel laughs, "Sorry Mike, my baby sister is usually not here on the weekends, so she's not used to you yet." Rachel opens the door and lets him in with the boys as she pulls me to her room. "Rachel, who are those two boys with momma's friend and how you know his name?" I was confused as I peeked out the door. "Mia, that's momma's new boyfriend. He's been coming over for the last couple of weekends when you have been with Andre, and during the week after you go to bed. I guessed those are his two sons, Ryan and Tim, he's always talking about, but don't you worry about that you're too young to understand. Plus he'll probably be gone in a minute like her other two friends before him." I quickly turned around and said, "Rachel, I will be seven years old, so I am not a baby anymore." Rachel laughed hugging me.

I went and started playing with my dolls while waiting for my dad to come. I ended up falling asleep because my dad was just taking too long today. When I woke up, I knew that he should have been here by now. I ran into Rachels room crying "Ray, can you call my daddy he should have been here by now." Rachel hugged me tightly, she hated to see me cry, "He came when you were sleep, and momma told him you weren't going this weekend because she had plans for you." Broken hearted I couldn't help but cry even more, "I want to go with my daddy!" Momma didn't get why I loved my daddy so much. I guess that came with her not knowing who her father was. She walked into the room as Rachel was hugging me, "Mia girl shut that noise up. Your daddy is over there with that woman and any other woman he can get with. He's not thinking about you. Besides you need to spend some time with your soon to be step-dad and step-brothers." "Step-dad?" me and Rachel both screamed together.

I looked up at Rachel, and the look of shock on her face let me know she didn't have a clue about the news she just heard either. "Mom, what are you talking about?" Rachel asked with confusion in her voice. "So, what you two think Andre is the only one who can move on and get married? I am going to show him that I can move on too." I guess she felt she had something to prove to everyone because she wasn't married and my dad was. "But momma you don't even know this man you've only known him for a couple of months," Rachel told our mom as I just stood there. "Oh, so it was okay for Andre to marry someone in weeks, but not me." Momma said as she walked off. Rachel waited until mom walked off and looked over at me, "Marriage isn't a game. Don't ever get married just to get back at someone. Marry for love and stability" Rachel was only fifteen, but she knew something wasn't right, and this was all moving very quickly, but she also decided not to say anything. She was glad that my mom was finally happy even if the situation was moving too fast for her, she didn't want our mom to think she wasn't happy for her.

Four days after my 7th birthday my mom and Mike got married. I guess I was happy the day of the wedding because I got to wear a pretty dress. After the wedding ceremony, they had a big reception and we all dance, partied, ate and had a good time. While everyone was dancing Mike's, older son came over to me and smiled I smiled back and waved. "I am going to be around a lot more now that my dad and your mom are married." I laughed because he talked funny. He lived around a lot of white rich folks and he went to school with their kids, so he was very proper when he spoke. The rest of the night at the reception I would catch Ryan, Mike's oldest son, just looking at me. I didn't like it at all. I spotted Rachel and ran over to her, "Ray Mike's son is weird, he keeps looking at me and watching me." Rachel laughed and said, "Mia you know them boys weird, they don't have a lot of black people where they live so they may just be shocked with the music and stuff." Rachel and I laughed and started back dancing together. That night when we went home, everyone was one big happy family.

# LIFE CHANGED FOREVER

**She sits staring at the wall in disbelief.**
**She couldn't understand what just took place.**
**Not knowing what to do she runs and hides.**
**Feeling alone and abused, she doesn't know what to do.**
**She was only seven years old and couldn't understand.**
**Her smile and laugh would never be the same**
**The pain she feels will forever remain.**
**Her innocence was stolen.**
**Just Snatched Away...**

My mom and Mike had been married for a year now, and things were not going the way I thought they would. I was now spending less time with my dad and felt like I was being forced to spend more time with this new family that my mom and Mike had created. I didn't get married so why did I have to be a part of this. I just couldn't understand why I was not able to go with my dad on weekends anymore. "Mia we will see," is the only responds my dad would give me. He never would say anything wrong about my mom. When I would ask my dad what was going on, all he would say is ask my mom. Every time I would ask her I would get the same answer just in a different way.

"Ma, I want to go with my daddy this weekend please," I begged her as we were driving home. I looked over and caught her rolling her eyes as she would normally do before she said with an attitude, "Girl your daddy doesn't have time for you. He's too busy living and doing what he wants to do. You see he don't do nothing for you." No matter how much my mom told me that he didn't care I never believed her. She never had anything good to say about my dad since they were not together anymore. Deep down in my heart, I knew my dad cares and loves me, and no one could make me think differently. Anytime momma called him for money he would bring it with no problem. "That's not true my daddy loves me, he just works a lot now that's all" I answered back as she was looking out the window. I always felt the need to defend my dad, because I loved him, and he was my dad. "Yeah, ok you will see eventually," my mom replied and ended the conversation at least for that day.

Later that evening when Mike came home he had his two sons with him as he did every weekend. Ryan who was now 16 and Tim who was 14. I didn't like them too much, and they had nothing in common with me, but I wasn't the type to be mean for no reason, so I spoke and went to watch tv. As it got later and later I realize that once again I would be at home. I didn't think it was fair that Mike had his kids and I couldn't go with my dad, but I was a child, so it wasn't much I could do about it.

I went to my room to get ready for bed. Laying in bed watching one of my favorite shows I could feel someone looking at me. I jumped up and screamed realizing it was just one of my step-brothers. "Ryan, why are you standing at my door just staring at me?", I asked as I laid back down pulling the cover tight around my neck. I didn't trust him. He just looks sneaky, and nothing about him was normal. "Oh nothing," Ryan said as he just walked away as if it was nothing wrong with him just standing in the dark watching me. "He's so weird," I said to myself.

The next day I asked again, "Can you please call my daddy to come get me, please?" My mom just ignored my plead and went on to say what she was going to say as if she didn't even hear me talking. "Mike and I have some things to do. Rachel is outside with Tim and her friends, so Ryan is going to stay in the house with you." I didn't like that suggestion, "Momma, I don't know that boy I don't want to stay here with him. Plus he's weird." She laughed, "Mia, that's your step-brother you know them stop being a brat and spend some time with your new brother." She knew I didn't like when anybody called them my brothers. I walked away "They are not my brothers."

An hour after Mike and my mom left Ryan walked into my room while I was playing with my dolls. I looked up and decided to be nice, so I ask, "do you want to play with me?" Holding a doll out for him to play with it. Ryan sat down and grabbed a doll. He played with me for a little while before throwing the doll on the bed. "Ok, I played with you now you have to play my game with me." I had no clue what I was getting myself into when I agreed to play Ryan's game.

"So what is this game and how do you play?", I asked. "The game is called Body parts," Ryan said as I looked confused. "What kind of game is this? I know all my body parts. So, this game should be easy.", I had never heard of this game before. I just thought it was something him and his friends played only in his neighborhood. "Good so you should be able to win this game," Ryan said and smiled. It was something about the way he smiled I didn't like, but I went ahead and played with him anyway just to show my mom I was trying to get along with him. Hoping that would get her to let me go to my dad's house. "So, how do you play this game?", I was ready to get this over with before it even started. "I will call out body parts on either my body or yours, and you have to point to it or touch it with whatever body part called before the one you are on," Ryan explain the rules to me. I did not like the rules of this game, "No, I'm not playing, and I'm not touching you. You must be crazy." Ryan laughed and told me, "Stop acting like a baby, I thought you were a big girl." He knew I didn't like being called a baby and figure that would get me to do what he wanted, and he was right for now. I went ahead and played the game against what I felt was a terrible idea, "I'll play with you."

Ryan started the game by calling out little simple body parts so that I could get comfortable. Just like he expected I was beginning to feel better about the game. Ryan calls out right hand, and I held my right hand with my left hand. The game quickly starts to change after the next body part was called. He said, "penis," which means I would have to put my right hand on his penis. I didn't understand what was going on at that moment or what he was saying for me to do. I kind of understood, but I wasn't about to do it, "What are you saying Ryan, I can't do that," before I knew it he grabs my right hand. I tried to pull away, but his grip was so tight it was hard for me to pull away. He put my hand on his penis, and I screamed, "That's nasty, let my hand go! I am not playing with you anymore, and I'm going to tell Rachel what you did." I finally got my hand out of his pants and ran into my sister's room. I thought Rachel would be inside by now, but she wasn't, so I closed the door. That was the nastiest thing I had ever felt.

A few minutes pass, and I heard a knock on the door. "Mia, come on it was just a game," Ryan yelled through the door. "Besides that's what men and women do when they like each other," he then added. The only problem is I was only a seven-year-old little girl. My mom had never talked to me about what to do if something like this happens, so I did not know what to do or even if this was normal, but I just felt in my heart that it wasn't right. I waited a couple of minutes before opening the door, and telling him "I am never touching you again." Ryan assured me that wouldn't have to touch him again. Once Ryan made sure I was back comfortable and relaxed, he knew he wanted to get me to play the game more, he wasn't done just yet. "Well, we have to keep playing to get a winner, and this time it's my go. I'll call out things for me to do, and you can make sure I don't cheat." Rolling my eyes, and ready for him to get out my room I said, "Just hurry up so I can go play with my dolls."

Ryan started calling out things, and in a blink, he was pulling my pants down with one hand over my mouth and the other between my legs. I kicked and moved from the pain, but no matter how much I pushed he wouldn't budge, It seems Ryan liked seeing me in pain. I felt his penis becoming larger on my leg, and I didn't like that. I kicked, tried screaming and biting his hand that was covering my mouth. He quickly pulled his pants down and began to stick his penis between my legs. I started feeling pain like I had never felt. Before Ryan was able to go any further in me, I finally bit his hand which caused him to lose his balance, and I ran as fast as I could across the house to Rachels room screaming and locking the door before Ryan could catch up to me. "Mia, you can't tell your mom because if you do, you'll never be able to go with your dad again. We all know how much you love your dad. So, you better not tell anyone." I heard Ryan say as I put a pillow over my head.

I woke up to Rachel standing over me asking was I hungry? Remembering what I just experience before falling asleep. I felt dirty and disgusting, so I ran to the bathroom jumping in the tub. After scrubbing my body for what seemed like forever, I finally felt like I was clean enough to get out the tub. Coming out of the bathroom, to everyone sitting in the kitchen eating and laughing, made me angry. I was still in a bad mood from what had taken place earlier that day. "What's so funny, and why is everybody so happy?" I asked because I wasn't in the mood to laugh or even be sitting down at the table with them. I went ahead and sat down. My mom turned to me and smiled, "Ryan told me you both had a good time today." In disgust, I threw my pizza back in the box and said, "Well Ryan is a lie, and I am not staying anywhere with him ever again." Everyone just sat at the table looking confused as I walked out the kitchen and into my room. I heard my mom finally say, "Maybe she's just mad because she couldn't go with her dad, she will be ok." Ryan quickly added, "Yes she was talking about him all day she really loves her dad." "Why don't you tell them the truth," I screamed from my room, but I don't think anyone heard me because the door was close.

Sunday didn't come fast enough for me; I was ready to get those boys away from me and back to where they came from. More Ryan than Tim. Sunday evening came, and everyone was saying their goodbyes and see you later to the boys except for me. I didn't care if I ever saw them again. My mom motion for me to come over, "Mia come tell Ryan and Tim bye. The train is almost here for them." I mumble, "It needs to hurry up and hit Ryan on the way up," as I walked over. Looking at Tim, and then at Ryan and with the meanest voice, I could ever get I said, "Bye" and walked back to get in the car.

Mike asked Ryan, "What did you do to her?" Ryan was a little scared he thought his dad knew something, but he wasn't sure, so he smiled and said, "Dad I didn't do anything." Mike looked at Ryan, and he could tell Ryan was lying, but I'm sure he had no clue that his son was a child molester. He let it go and not too long after the train came, and they were on their way back to their mother's house, to their everyday life. While I was left with so many unanswered questions and unwanted feelings and emotions that I had not ever felt. I was upset with my mom because she left me home with this boy. I was disappointed with my dad for not picking me up as he should have even if my mom told him no he should have fought harder to get me and mad at Mike for bringing Ryan into my life.

Monday morning while getting ready for school. I went to talk to my mom. I went to her room after Mike left for work. "Ma, are boys supposed to be putting they private parts into girl's private?"

She looked shocked at the question, "Mia you are too young to be worried about that. You better go to school and get good grades." I didn't understand, if mom is saying I am too young even to be talking like this, why did Ryan do what he did to me, I thought to myself. "So, it's not okay for boys to do that is it?" I asked trying to get a clear understanding, but I got nothing. "Mia go get dress for school you are too young to be talking about that type of stuff." My mom told me, and I finished getting ready for school and got on the school bus.

I got on the bus and spotted my best friend, Chari. I sat down next to her like I did every day. Chari and I were so close everyone thought and believed that we were cousins. It wasn't too hard to convince people because we were always together, and we had the same last name. Chari had no idea what happened to me over the weekend, and I didn't know if I should tell anyone. Noticing Chari had a new pair of shoes, "I like your shoes Chari," I hurried up and said something before Chari could ask me about my weekend. I didn't want to have to lie to Chari because I never lied or kept secrets from anyone up until this point. I was told always tell the truth even if it meant I would get in trouble. "Thank you Mia, my mom bought them yesterday." Chari started telling me about her weekend, and by the time she got ready to ask me about mine, it was time for us to get off the bus and go to class. So my plan to change the conversation worked, so instead of lying to anyone I'll just change the subject.

After school on the bus ride home Chari asked me was I ok, and I said I was, but Chari didn't believe me, and I knew she didn't. "Mia, you know you can tell me anything," Chari grabbed my hand as we rode home. Chari could tell I was not myself, but she just sat next to me holding my hand, as I held back tears in my eyes.

# *LESS & MORE*

I started to spend and see my dad less and being touched and used more. I tried telling my mom a couple of times, but she was so caught up in her own life she didn't even realize what I was trying to say to her. The last time I tried to talk about it to her, I'm told that only fast girls would be thinking about that type of stuff at my age. So, I kept holding on to this secret and was too scared to tell anyone because I didn't want to be label the "grown girl" momma was talking about. I was the kind sweet girl, and I tried to keep it that way. I learned to hide and keep all my feelings and anger inside.

This week I was excited, and that was a feeling I had not felt in a long time. My birthday was coming up, and my dad promised me he would be there to pick me up no matter what that Friday. All week I thought about Friday because I had not spent a weekend with my dad and Tamara in over three months. I missed them, but I was able to call them both every day, and I did just that. Friday came, and as he promises, he was there to pick me up.

"Mia, your dad is here," I heard my momma yelled with

an attitude from the front door. "Hi daddy," I screamed running to the door with so much excitement. I was still a daddy's girl no matter how mad I would get with him for not picking me up all the time like he used to, and no matter what my mom would say about him. I went to get in the car and saw my step-mom Tamara, I got even more excited. I loved my bonus-mom so much. I didn't like the word step-mom because our relationship was different. We had a special bond that you usually don't see between a step-mother and step-daughter. Tamara was far from the wicked step-mother that most kids get. She would do anything for me and treated me like I was one of her kids she gave birth to if not better. Tamara kids were older than me and my dad's other kids so she could love us without anyone feeling jealous, and her three kids even loved me just as much especially my sister, Sherell which was Tamara's middle child. And only when I got ready to get in the car I saw my two older sisters India and Toya, my dad had them previously, before meeting my mom. I knew from that moment this weekend was going to be one of the best weekends ever.

Super excited when I got in the car would be an understatement. My sisters had the same mom, so they stayed together. I always felt like they were closer and shared a better relationship together then they had with me. I guess overall we all had a great bond and was very close, they were just closer. That night we all went to dinner and a movie. "Since it's Mia's birthday you get to pick the movie, Mia," Tamara told us on the drive to the movie theater. I whispered to my sisters, "What movie yall want to see?" I would never decide by myself when we were all together. We all said the same thing as if we planned it and the three of us laughed as we got out of the car.

Saturday morning, we woke up to the house decorated

for the party Tamara had planned. We ate breakfast as some family and friends came over to celebrate my birthday with me. It was a pool party, so we went and got in the pool. I loved the pool, and my sisters did too. We could be in the pool all day if you let us. I was enjoying myself and having so much fun that for a second I forgot about the reality of what probably was going to happen when I got home that night.

We got out the pool and went back into the house. The food was ready, so we ate, and Tamara had brought out a big cake for me. Everyone sang happy birthday, and Tamara cut the cake for everyone to eat. I ran and hugged Tamara thanking her so much for everything. It started getting later in the night, so we begged Tamara to ask could we stay until tomorrow since it was only Saturday and we usually go home on Sundays anyway. Tamara talks daddy into letting us stay another night, and we played and laughed the rest of the night away.

That next afternoon when dropping India and Toya off while waiting in the car with Tamara, I asked, "Tamara can I come stay with you and my dad?" which caught Tamara off guard because I had never asked that before. "Mia, I think your mom will miss you too much if you leave her." I mumble, "I doubt it, and I sure won't miss living in that house." Tamara heard a little of what I said, but my dad was getting back into the car, so she didn't want to say anything to let him know how I was feeling until she was able to talk to me and find out what was going on.

Not too long after we were pulling up to my house, and I started to cry. I hated the sight of my own home. If only people knew what was going on inside that house, I thought to myself. Hell, the people living in the house didn't even know what was going on in the walls of their home. Daddy promises me that he would be back to get

17

me that Friday if I stop crying, and that just wasn't good enough for me. After a couple of minutes of convincing, Tamara had finally talk me into going into the house. Daddy carried the box with the rest of my cake to the door while I grab the rest of my gifts and things. My mom was waiting at the door, and when she saw us walking up, she opened the door with an attitude. She snatched the cake from my dad as he was handing it to me to take into the house. As my mom snatches the cake she yells, "She can't carry that why would you give her that?" and pushes my dad which causes the cake to fall to the ground. I looked over at my cake, and it was ruined. I knew my mom wouldn't do anything to hurt me on purpose, but it seems like my mom was never thinking about how things would affect me, only thinking about herself in the moment. "What is wrong with you Lisa?" Andre asked as he grabs her hand to avoid her hitting him. "You're my problem, I told you not to bring that lady to my house," Lisa said snatching her hand away. I couldn't believe what was happening. I ran to Rachel to tell her what happen to my cake. Rachel hugged me and asked did I have a good weekend to try to cheer me up. Rachel began to tell me what she did over the weekend, and before she knew it, I was back happy again.

Next Friday came, and of course, my mom didn't let me go with my dad because she had plans for me since I went with him last weekend for my birthday. I was upset but wasn't too mad because I was going to be able to celebrate my birthday two weeks in a row. To my surprise, we didn't do anything at all. Mike came home with the boys, and they watched a movie and ate a pizza, and that was pretty much it for Friday night, and that was the routine every Friday night I was home. That Saturday when I woke up my mom and Mike were gone to the store and Rachel was sleep, but the boys were up. I walked into the kitchen not saying anything to them. "Mia, I have a birthday gift for you," Tim said to me. I was excited because I loved getting gifts and feeling special. "Really what did you get me," I asked. "I'll give it to you after you eat your breakfast," Tim said as he sat down to finish eating his breakfast.

Later that morning, while I was in my room playing and watching tv, Tim came in and asked me, was I ready for my gift. I jumped up saying yes. I didn't have any bad feelings toward Tim because he was always nice and never did anything to me, unlike his nasty older brother. "Ok, we are going to play hiding seek, and I'm going to hide with your gift, and you have to find me," Tim told me. I felt comfortable with playing with him, so I agreed, "First I need to change my clothes because I can't run with a dress." I started to look for something else to put on. "Oh it's okay we are just going to play in the house we are not going outside or anything," Tim said to me. "I guess you are right." We begin to play. Tim went to hide in my mom's closet because it was a huge closet. It would be easy to hide in there, and he knew that was my favorite hiding spot from when we played hiding seek before. So, the first place that I would look was in my mom's closet. At first, I didn't see Tim because he was deep in the closet, but as I walked into the closet, I spotted him. "Yes, I found you now where is my birthday gift?" I was excited because I wanted my gift. Tim grabbed me and pulled me toward him laughing and out of nowhere he kissed me in my mouth as he put his hand in my panties. Not again, not you too is all I could think as I tried to pull away, but Tim was a big kid for his age, and I was only ten years old so no matter how much I tried to get away I just couldn't move around in the closet like I wanted to. Finally when he saw I didn't like what he was doing he let me go. "So you only like it when

Ryan does it to you, well maybe you will like this," Tim said to me as he tried to put his hands back in my pants, but was quickly stop when Rachel screams, "Mia, where are you?", Tim let me go, and I ran as fast as I could to Rachel. "Get dress you are going with me," Rachel told me as she walked to my room to pick out my clothes.

We went out leaving those boys home. Having sister's day with Rachel's best friend Shawn and her sister Karen was always fun. I was the baby of the bunch because of the age gap between Rachel and me, but Rachel didn't mind, and she loved taking me with her, or maybe my mom made her take me. Whatever the case she always treated me right. We went to the mall and then to the movies while at the mall Rachel asked me, "What were you doing in momma's closet before we left the house earlier?" I looked away as I tried to explain, "I was supposed to be playing hide and seek, with Tim, but when I went to find him, he was hiding in momma's closet. I went into the closet to get him, and he…" before I could finish telling Rachel what happen Shawn called her from the fitting room to see if Rachel liked the outfit she was trying on. I had finally built up the courage to tell what's been going on, but my chance was gone in a blink of an eye. Rachel pulled me over to the fitting room with her, and that ended that conversation between us. We never spoke of it again. I knew that I would probably never build up the courage to tell anyone again, but I couldn't take any more abuse from one person, now I have to worry about two.

After Rachel took me to get something to eat, we headed home. When we got back to the house, my mom was there alone, and Mike had taken the boys out. "Mia, did you have fun hanging out with the big girls today?" I smiled and shook my head, "Yes momma I had a good time. Rachel brought me something for my birthday, and we went to the movies." Showing my mom, the toy that Rachel and her two friends got me as a birthday gift. Rachel looking around asked, "Where's Mike and the boys at?" "Gone for good I hope," I said before I even realize I was talking. "Mia, you still don't like Mike what's with you? I thought you liked Mike now you don't again," Rachel asked laughing. I actually like Mike he was always nice to me and willing to do anything for me, but because Ryan and Tim were his kids, I begin to grow a dislike for him because of them. "Mike isn't the problem. It's his kids I hate." I was filled with anger anytime they came up. Rachel laughed even harder, thinking that I was just mad because my dad hadn't been picking me up as much since the boys came into the picture. Not knowing that they were touching and molesting her little sister. "Mia don't talk like that and Rachel stop laughing at her. That's not funny." My mom screamed at both of us which only made Rachel laugh harder. "I'm serious momma I want them boys gone even if that means Mike has to go too." I said, as Rachel finally was able to stop laughing and look over at me, "Mia they go home every Sunday when they are here. So, you only see them maybe a day, two days if you put that Friday they get here together with that Sunday morning before they leave." "Well that's too long for me. I don't want to see them ever, and I wish momma would stop making me stay here to spend time with them. They are not my brothers, and they will never be." I told Rachel and momma as I walked into my room. That night I had to deal with Ryan sneaking into my room as I did every Saturday night.

It had been weeks since Tim had begun touching me. It seemed like he was pressured into doing this. One Saturday I heard him and Ryan at my door, "You better get in there and do it or else I'm going to beat you up when we get home." Ryan told Tim, "But I don't like touching on her,"

Tim tried to tell Ryan. "If you don't do it I am going to tell everybody you are gay just like they think you are," right after Ryan threating to tell everybody Tim was gay, Tim came into my room.

My body was not the same anymore, and neither was I. Now they would take turns coming into my room while everyone was sleep or when our parents would leave us home. They were monsters that had to be stop. I couldn't talk to my mom because she didn't want to listen all she was worried about was her perfect little family and not doing anything to ruin it. So, I had to come up with a plan to get out of this nightmare I was thrown into.

# ESCAPE PLAN

I knew that Rachel and my mom didn't understand why I was so angry because they weren't the ones getting touched on and treated like someone sex slave. I had to figure out something, so I decided that I would start spending more time away from home. I just had to figure out who I would use to help me escape. Since my mom was so angry and bitter with my dad, I couldn't use him because I could barely get over to his house when I was supposed to so I knew anything extra was out the question.

"Chari!", I shouted out loud. That's who she'll let me go with and not have a problem. Mom had already allowed Chari's dad and mom to take me on Wednesday after school because we always wanted to do something together and she would be working late. I knew that if someone else is in my room at night with me, the boys wouldn't come in there and mess with me and risk the chances of them getting caught. They wanted everybody to believe they were good boys, but in reality, they were molesters.

Monday came around, and I was so excited to put my plan in motion. I got on the bus and spoke to the bus

23

driver, "Hi, Ms. Highsmith, how are you?" as I walked pass Ms. Highsmith smiled and waved then speaking to the bus aide as I did every morning and after school... "Hi, Ms. Angie, I like your hair." Ms. Angie smiled at me and said thank you, as she handed me a bag of candy like she did every morning. See I had a way of winning people over because even though I was hiding a terrible secret, I was one of the sweetest, smartest, and prettiest little girls you could ever meet. I would always smile and talk to everyone. I wanted everyone to feel important and loved even if at times I wasn't sure if I was any of that.

"Chari do you want to spend the night over at my house this weekend?" I said as I sat down. "Sure, well first I have to ask my momma," Chari said with excitement. That day when I got home, I was so happy because Chari's mom, Auntie Tangie, as I call her, had called and spoke with my mom. She said it was ok for me to spend the night over at their house that weekend if momma didn't mind, and the following weekend Chari could come over with me. Just like that, my plan was starting to work.

One weekend while at Chari's house I meet one of Chari's neighbors who had not too long moved into the neighborhood. "Mia this is Ronyette, she just moved around here. Ronyette this is my cousin Mia." Chari said as we walked over to Ronyette as she was sitting on her porch. That day Ronyette, Chari, and I laugh and play together. I gained another great friend thanks to Chari.

For the next two years, Chari and I rotated going to each other's houses on the weekends. When Chari was away at her dad's or grandma's house, I would be able to go over to my dad's house, and I even started going over to my sisters India and Toya's house as well. So, I was barely home to see Ryan and Tim, which I was just fine with.

A couple of weekends while Chari was over the

monsters had come to my room, and once they saw Chari was there, they would just leave out. "Mia, why do they always come to your room at night?" Chari asked one night after Ryan had peeked into the room realizing Chari was there and closed the door. "Because they're animals and I hate them," is all I told Chari because I was too scared to tell her the truth. I didn't want Chari to think that I liked what they were doing to me, so I decided not to tell her.

During the Christmas break, I got stuck in the house with the two people I had grown to hate being around. My mom and step-dad decided to do some last-minute Christmas shopping for us, and Rachel had to work. I figure I'll go into my room to stay away from them. I closed the door and started watching TV hoping that I would not have to deal with them today, but I knew it had been awhile since they had been able to mess with me. Since I made it my business to stay gone every weekend I had not seen them in months. They both walked into my room one after the other and closed the door. Tim sat on the bed next to me, and I jumped up and moved closer to the wall. As I was trying to move closer to the wall, Ryan hurried and sat on the other side of me putting me in the middle of them both. I knew this was not going to be good. I wasn't seven or eight anymore I was older now, so I figured out that Ryan had told Tim what he had been doing to me, which is when he started making Tim do it too. For the first time in a long time, I felt afraid and alone. I had been avoiding them for so long now I forgot about the reality of what could happen if I was ever home with them again.

"Mia, we missed you. You are never home anymore, and we don't have anyone here to play with when you are gone." Ryan said as he moved closer to me. Tim didn't say much from the looks of things he was just following his older brother's lead. I looked over at him, and for some reason, he didn't look like he wanted to be in there, The same way he looks most of the times he came in my room. For whatever reason, my heart allowed me to kind of feel bad for him for just a moment, remembering all the other times that Tim was along and touching me while Ryan listens and watched at the door to make sure he was doing what he told him to do. I realize that he may also be a victim of Ryan as well, but I didn't really care I had to figure out how to help myself at this point.

I was knocked out of my thoughts when something was jammed into my face and then in my mouth. I began to choke and then I realize Ryan had put his dick into my mouth. I had never had this done to me, and I was so humiliated that I started to cry, but the tears I cried this day were filled with anger and raged. I looked around, and Tim was nowhere to be found, he had run out of the room once Ryan started to attempt to make me give him oral sex. I bit him, and he screams, but I didn't let go. He finally was able to pull his dick out the grip of my teeth, and he ran out my room in pain. I had had enough.

Not long after my mom and step-dad came back in with food, but I didn't move from my bed or room. I stayed in there for the rest of the night and half of the next morning. Rachel walked into asked was I ok. I just laid there and motion yes with my head. The rest of my break would only be a blah to me. I didn't enjoy my Christmas even though I was giving everything I asked for and more. I acted as if I was happy and excited because I really wanted to be, but deep-down I was dealing with controlling my rage, I was ready to kill somebody, these secrets were making me become someone I didn't want to be.

New Years was approaching, and I overheard Rachel and her friends talking about New Year's Resolutions.

"Ray, what are New Year's Resolutions?" I asked my sister. "It's something you want to change for the New Year that you did the previous year." Rachel motion for me to sit down as she continues, "For example, say you don't like being skinny, and then you would say, my new year's resolution is to gain weight for the new year." "So, it's anything I don't like about this year I say I'm going to change it and then what?" I asked because I was still a little confused. "Then you do whatever it is you have to do to make the change," Rachel told me as she walked away. I'm going to get rid of them for good this year, I promised myself. I promise myself that I will not go through another year of this.

# AFTER ALL THESE YEARS

It was a new year, and things were changing all around me. Chari wouldn't be going to the same middle school as me. Rachel was going off to college, and for some strange reason, my dad was coming around more especially when Mike was not at home. I only had two weeks before middle school, and I was very nervous. I knew that a lot of the kids from my class would be there, but it would be the first time I would be going to school without my best friend, and I didn't like that. Chari helped me escape from a lot of things, and she didn't even know any of it was going on. I was afraid that Chari would meet new people and forget all about me.

Rachel had already gone off to college up in Atlanta. She promised me that she would call and check on me every day after she got out of class. Rachel had been keeping her promise every day since she left, but I missed my sister.

The weekend before I was to start school my mom and Mike decided that the boys would come over the same weekend I would be home. But, things were going to be different because I had a plan and was ready for them this weekend. I wasn't sure if Ryan had learned his lesson when

I tried to rip his dick off with my teeth. So, just in case he didn't learn I had a plan this time around. Mike and the boys came into the house as I was finishing up my food. I looked at them and smiled which was not usual for me to smile at them, and it caught them by surprise.

Once no one was paying attention I put a butcher knife under my shirt and walked into my room. I closed the door and took the knife and placed it under my pillow. I waited for my mom and Mike to close their door and get ready for bed. I knew once their door was locked it was only a matter of time before one of the boys came to try and make there move, and I was ready for them tonight. I knew that it would more than likely be Ryan because it was almost always him. "Tonight, will be the last night they ever put a hand on me," I said out loud as I just laid in bed looking at the ceiling.

As I predicted an hour after hearing my mom's and Mike door closed my door slowly started opening. My hand already under the pillow on the knife. I waited for a body to pop up and I was praying it was Ryan because although Tim had also touched me, he didn't do anything else, but Ryan, that bastard had no limits to what he would do to me and what he would try to make me do to him. As I laid in bed acting like I was watching TV, out the corner of my eyes, I saw a tall shadow, and I knew it was Ryan. Yes, my prayers are being answered. He got closer, and I grabbed the knife tight. As soon as he started to sit down on the bed next to me, I pulled the knife out and pointed it right at his neck. I really didn't know what I was going to do, but I was willing to do whatever needed to be done for him to never put his filthy hands or body on me again. I saw the fear in Ryan's eyes for once I felt powerful, and I knew that I was no longer a weak little girl that he once ruled, used, and abused.

"Mia, what are you doing I was just coming to say hi.", Ryan said with fear running all through his voice. "Yeah, sure you were like all the other nights you were just coming to say hi, but ended up either on top of me or putting your hands in places that I didn't want them to be," I said pushing the knife closer to him. I finally felt like I was in charge of what was going to happen for once. "It doesn't feel good not being in control, does it?" I laughed and moved the knife toward him more. "get out of here and don't you ever come back in here before I stab you in your throat." Ryan ran out the room, and I laid looking at the ceiling feeling more powerful than ever.

Monday came, and I started my new journey as a pre-teen in middle school. I had so many emotions coming over me at one time. I meet two girls that week in school, and we bonded. Nikki and Tanari where best friends from elementary school. Once we started a friendship, we were inseparable. Middle school wasn't as bad as I thought it would be without Chari because I would still talk to her every day and go over on the weekends. No matter who I became friends with no one could ever replace Chari.

I am sitting in health class, and the topic is sex education. I was interested because now I was finally going to be able to get the answers that I had been curious about for the last couple of years, but boy I was not ready for what I thought I heard my teacher say. I begin to pay close attention. "Ms. Hicks can you repeat what you just said, please," I asked. "Sure Mia, I was saying if someone is touching you or forcing themselves on you and you are asking them to stop, that person is committing a crime. That crime is called a couple of things. Two of them could be sexual assault, or it could be rape." Ms. Hicks repeated. I waited a while so that I wouldn't draw attention to myself before asking to used the bathroom. I ran to the bathroom and began to cry and scream. "So, all these years I've been getting raped and sexually assaulted, and no one told me. No one tried to help me. All I knew was only grown girls think about that type of stuff!" I said to the mirror in front of me. I felt stupid and angry, but this time I was going to make everyone who I thought was supposed to protect me, and didn't pay. For what I went through nobody was safe, and everyone had to pay. I dried up my tears and put a smile back on my face, because that is what I was used to doing. No one ever saw me cry and I liked it that way. As I was walking out of the bathroom, Nikki was walking in. "Hey Mia, you ok?" Nikki asked as she went into the bathroom. "I will be okay soon," I said and walked out the door before Nikki could respond.

I was angry at almost everyone in my family. Middle school taught me so much about life. I figured out so much that I had been so blind to for so many years. I found out that my mom and dad was having an affair together for the past year. Neither one of them thought that I knew about them sleeping together behind their husband and wife back, but I knew. My dad started picking me up in the mornings dropping me off to school, but that was just an excuse he gave so that he wouldn't get caught for what he was really over there for.

Every morning when it was time for me to get up my dad would already be there in my mom's room. I continue to act like I didn't know what was going on and I was still the little girl that was clueless. One morning I heard Tamara outside screaming. I peeked out the window and saw Tamara wiping away tears. I then realize that my step-mom was hurt for knowing that my dad and mom was messing around again. I didn't like to see Tamara hurt, but I didn't mind seeing Mike hurt because if it wasn't for him, I would have never been raped and sexually assaulted.

On Friday Mike was going to be dropping me off at my sister's house for the weekend, and I decided on the ride over I would tell him about my mom and dad's affair. While riding, I turned to Mike and asked, "Do you know my daddy and momma are sleeping together?" Mike was surprised at what he just heard, "Mia, what are you talking about where did you get that from? When does this happen?" Mike was so confused. He knew I had been acting and treating him different lately, so I think he thought I was just making this all up. "Don't believe me huh, well why don't you call Tamara and asked her. See you later." I said as I was getting out of the car and running into my sisters house.

When I got back home, my mom asked, "What did you tell Mike" I looked at her and simply said, "the truth" and walked into my room. I wasn't expecting her to follow me, but she did, "Mia, why would you tell him that I'm seeing your dad, that's not true. Are you trying to ruin my marriage?" I looked at her "Your marriage ruined my life." as I sat on the bed and started watching TV. See I started not liking my mom when she kept brushing me off every time I would try to talk to her about what had been going on. So, I could care less about her marriage. "This girl....," she said as she turned and walked out my room.

Mike came to me later that week. "Mia, I talked to your step-mom, and she told me everything." I smiled "I know she did" and I walked off. I hated Mike not because of who he was, but because of what his kids did to me. Since I couldn't hurt them, I wanted their dad to suffer.

I started to talk back to Mike and not do what he told me to do. I figured if telling him that my mom and dad were sleeping together couldn't get him to leave, I'll just be as mean as I can be to him and then he'll never speak to me again, and one-day one of us would be gone. Mike couldn't understand what was happening. He always had a great relationship with me. "Mia, what's wrong what happen to you?" Mike would ask me, and I would only respond with a simple "YOU!"

# THE CONFESSION

It was close to the end of the school year, and I was enjoying middle school. I was the girl that all the boys thought was cool to hang with and the girls thought was a cool friend to have. A lot of the boys had a crush on me, but that was as far as it went. Don't get me wrong a liked the attention, and because of my friendship with a lot of boys, some of the girls had something against me. I learned to stop caring what people would think especially when they didn't know me. I didn't understand what the problem was with being friends with boys. I talked to everyone that spoke to me it was just that simple to me.

However, there was this one boy that liked me, and I kind of liked him too. His name was Anthony, but everyone called him Lil Tony. He was tall and had nice brown eyes. It was something about the way he carried himself that I liked. He was a bad boy, and I was still considered a good girl. "So, you gone be my girlfriend?" Lil Tony said as he walked me to my class. I smiled and walked into the classroom without ever answering his question. I had never had a boyfriend, so this was going to be different for me. Yeah, I had boys that liked me before, but I was only in middle school. Plus I was always afraid of boys that liked me. The night before I had talked to Rachel and she said it was ok to have a boyfriend, but I could only speak on the phone with him and hang out in groups never alone. So I guess I'll give Lil Tony a chance.

"Nikki, I think I like Lil Tony, and I might be his girlfriend," I said as I couldn't stop smiling. "Girl that boy is crazy, but yall cute together. It's time you finally get a boyfriend." I was still unsure about the boyfriend thing. Later that day I saw Lil Tony again and knew he was going to ask me again. "So, you gone be my girlfriend or what man," Lil Tony asked while blocking me from walking. I smiled because I liked the way he took charged of the situation it was something about him that made me feel like he would protect me if I needed him to, and that was attractive to me. "Lil Tony, yes I'll be your girlfriend now move so I could go to class," I said as I pushed him to the side to continue walking.

Months had passed, and the school year was ending. Lil Tony and I were still dating. I became very close to his mother, Valencia. She is like a second mother to me. I call and talk to her on a daily and anytime I wanted to hang out she would come get me. As summer was starting, I knew that I would have to face those demons seeds that Mike and his ex-wife produce, most people called them my stepbrothers. Yeah, the knife scared them off for a little, but I wasn't sure if it would keep them away.

One day during the summer I just left the house and caught the bus to Lil Tony's house. I knew he wasn't there, but I wasn't going there for him anyway. I got off the bus and walked to the house by myself. "Hi, Ma is Lil Tony here?" I asked already knowing the answer was no. He had just called me before I left my house to head over there. Lil Tony would go to the projects where his grandmother lived on most weekends, and I knew that so him being home on the weekend was close to never. "Hi boo, no Lil Tony's not here, what's wrong with you Mia," Valencia asked as she opened the door for me to come in. I went in and sat down with Valencia. "I'm just not feeling good, and I hate being at my house," I said as I start to cry. I was not a crier, but I just was overwhelmed with guilt and mixed emotions I didn't know what else to do. "Don't cry boo, what's wrong? What happen? Did somebody touch you or bother you on the way here?" Valencia asked me as she hugged and rocked me in her arms. "Ma, I've been getting raped and sexually abused…. since I was seven years old and I've never told anyone because…. I was told that no one would believe me and that I would be looked at as the fast girl nobody would ever like…. I don't want…" before I could finish Valencia put her finger over my mouth, I moved her finger as I said "Please don't tell Lil Tony or anyone else. People already think they know stuff about me, but they don't know anything." I looked up at Valencia with a face full of hurt and tears. "You have to tell your mom Mia. You can't keep this from her she needs to know what's going on inside her house." Valencia told me drying my face. I didn't understand why it felt so good telling Valencia what was happening, and I hadn't told anyone up until this point. I just knew I could trust her not to judge me or blame me for what I had been through. I knew she was right I did need to tell my mom. "Ok, Ma, I'll tell her, but promise me you won't tell anybody." I felt embarrassed and ashamed as if I had done something wrong. "Boo, your secret is safe with me, but you have to tell your mom," Valencia told me again before she got ready to take me home. As Valencia and I rode home, that was the quietest ride we had ever had. "Mia, you didn't do anything wrong, and you have nothing to be ashamed of. You will always be my girl no matter what happens." Valencia told me as I got ready to get out of the car. I knew she meant every word she had said, but for some reason, I was full of shame and embarrassment.

Even though I had promised Valencia, I would tell my mom I had no intentions of telling her what happen that day. I was on my way to go spend the summer with Rachel away in college. I put on my happy face and walked into the house. "Mia where you been, girl?" Momma asked me. "Nowhere," I said, I didn't really tell momma much of what was going on with me because I didn't feel it matter to her. "Well, do you have everything ready to go we are leaving to take you up to Rachel in the morning," Momma said as she walked into my room checking to see what I had packed. This was the perfect time to tell her, but I wasn't ready to talk to her, it had to be on my time.

That summer was one of the best vacations I could ever remember having. While riding back home with Rachel and her friends, I was thinking about everything I had gone through, and I just wanted to start fresh. "I'm going to tell her," I thought out loud as I wrote a poem before I fell off to sleep. I started using writing as my escape because I was a very talented writer and that was the only way for me to express my feelings without any judgment.

When Rachel and I made it back to our house, it was late, and we both were tired. We walked into the house and saw Mike and his two sons watching TV. I instantly got an attitude, "Why are they still here?" I asked rolling my eyes. "Mia, what's wrong?" Rachel asked because she didn't understand my change of attitude, and I saw it all over her face. "Ray, I don't expect you to understand because you have no idea what's been going on," I said as I walked to my room and closed the door. "Ma, just let her get some rest she's probably tired." Rachel said stopping my mom from coming after me.

The next morning when I woke up, Mike and the boys were gone and so was Rachel. I felt this was the right time to finally talk to momma and tell her about everything that had been going on. I walked into her room, and for some reason, I felt nervous. "Ma, I need to talk to you and tell you something." I sat down on the bed. "What is it Mia.?" "Momma, Ryan, and Tim have been abusing me and touching me for a while now," I told her. I began to cry telling her all that I had been going through the last couple of years. She looked at me and asked, "Mia are you sure that's what's been happening? Have you told anybody else this? I don't think you should tell anyone else this until we are for sure this happened. And whatever you do, do not tell your daddy. It's not like he would care anyway." That was my mom's first responds to me. I couldn't believe it, no I am sorry this happen or I am going to call the police, nothing. I sat there for a minute before screaming "Did you not just hear what I told you and you asked me am I sure that this happened, what kind of mother are you?" I was heartbroken and in tears. At that moment, my feelings for my mother change. I was angry and so mad at her because she didn't protect me like I thought she would. She didn't even seem to care at all. I called Valencia, but Lil Tony answered the phone, "What's up baby?", he said. "Lil Tony where ma at," I asked I didn't even want to talk to him at this point. Besides he had a new girlfriend so I was still mad with him about that. "She's not here what's up?" Lil Tony asked me, but I just hung up the phone.

My godmother had just passed away, and she was the only other person I knew would believe me. "I wish my goddie was here." I thought to myself. I picked up the phone to call my god sister to talk to her. "Nicole, what are you doing?" I asked as Nicole answered the phone. "Nothing girl what you got going on," Nicole said, but she didn't sound normal something was different about her. I had been hearing people say things about her doing drugs, but I didn't believe them. People always started rumors, and half the time it was because they were jealous or had nothing else better to do. "Nicole, I need to tell you something. I've been getting sexually assaulted and abused by Mike's kids." I told Nicole as tears were still running down my face onto the pillow. "Did you tell Lisa or Andre about this... when did this happen... what did they say are they calling the police," Nicole asked concerned. "My mom asked me was I sure this had happened, and she told me not to tell anyone else until we're sure this happened," I was still in disbelief of her responds. "Mia let me call you right back when I figure out what's going on," Nicole said before hanging up.

A new school year started, and months went by before I heard back from Nicole, so when Nicole showed up to my school during dismissal, I was excited and shocked. "Mia, your momma said you can spend the weekend with me. I am going to take you home to get some clothes then you are going with me," Nicole told me as she motions for the man in the car with her to open the back door, so I could get in. Nicole looked different, but I thought it was because she had just had her first baby. "Why didn't my mom tell me that this morning before I left for school you were coming to get me," I asked getting into the car. "Because you were already gone when I called and talked to her." I just took Nicole's word for it because she had never lied to me before, and she had never given me a reason not to trust her. What I didn't know was that ever since my godmother died Nicole had been using drugs and getting

39

high.

Later that night while at Nicole's house getting ready for bed I heard the phone ring. Nicole and her two guy friends who had been riding around with us all day were in the living room. I overheard Nicole talking on the phone, "No, I haven't seen or heard from her in weeks. If I hear from her or I see her, I will call you." Then Nicole hangs up the phone. "Who was that on the phone, that sounded like my momma," I asked Nicole as she walked into the bedroom to check on me. "No that wasn't Lisa that was my friend looking for her daughter. She's always running away and usually would call me." Nicole told me as she walked back into the living room she turned back to me, "By the way Ben thinks you are cute." "That man is too old for me," I told Nicole as I frowned.

I ended up falling asleep and leaving Nicole and the guys in the living room. I was a light sleeper and would wake up to any noise I would hear because I got so used to the demons coming in my room. So when I heard the door open, I opened my eyes just enough to see, the guy Ben coming in. I laid there as if I was still sleeping because I knew Nicole wasn't going to let anything happen to me, at least that's what I thought. I saw him taking off his clothes and heading over to the bed. "So, what are you going to rape me too now!" I said as I still laid on the bed and it stops Ben in his tracks. "Rape you?" Ben seemed confused, "Nicole told me you were down for it and would do anything for her," Ben said as he sat on the end of the bed away from me with just his underwear on. "I have never forced myself on any chick and don't plan to start now." I laughed a little, "That's good to know, but Nicole is a lie, I have no clue on what y'all deal was, but I knew nothing about it." I told Ben as I pointed to his pants. He smiled and put his pants back on, "I guess she is going to have to pay me another way for the drugs I gave her." I jumped up "Drugs! Nicole doesn't do drugs what are you talking about boy?" I was shocked. "Babygirl you must not have been around your god sister lately. Your girl has been on that stuff since her mom was sick and when she died, it got worse." Ben told me as he put his pants back on and sat on the edge of the bed. "What you mean worse? Yeah, I knew she smoked weed every now and again, but that's it right?" I asked concerned even though I was just almost sold for some drugs. I always wanted to see the good in the people I loved. "Babygirl she's on that hard stuff, not just weed. You must not know anything about the drug game. If it was just weed, she wouldn't be trying to give you to me for no weed. Which, by the way, I am not going to touch you." Ben laughed as he put his shirt on. "No, I'm only 14 what do I need to know about the drug game. I don't do drugs," I said as I looked at Ben. He was kind of cute, and I liked that he didn't force me to do anything I didn't want to. "So why would Nicole think you would be so willing to sleep with me for her, you must've started having sex young," Ben said. I looked down as I answered, "I trusted Nicole with a secret, and she's trying to use it for her good. Trusting people hasn't been working too good for me, so I think I am just going to stop." I looked at Ben and said, "Hey, let me ask you something, does my mom really know I'm here." Mia just felt like her mom didn't know where she was. "Baby girl you have to ask your god sister that," Ben said as he laid on the floor. "I'm going to lay on this floor to make sure no one else comes in here to mess with you. I'm not the only dealer she may have promised you to." I smiled and said "Thanks." And Ben was right about three more dealers of Nicole's had tried to come into the room that night. And just like he promised he didn't let them in to get me. He paid them whatever Nicole owed them for them to leave me alone. For once someone was actually protecting me and that felt good.

The next morning, I asked Nicole to call my mom. "Mia, your mom already called I told her you were sleep, and she's gone to church now, so you'll just call her tonight." I no longer trusted her, so I didn't believe anything she told me after what almost happened last night. While I was getting dress to go home, I heard my mother's voice on the answering machine. "Hi Nicole if you see or hear from Mia please have her call me I'm worried about her, and I haven't heard or seen her. Andre is looking for her and…." Beeeeeep I heard before she could finish talking. We had been going through our issues, but I still loved my mom. I ran out the room, "You lied to me, you told me she said I could come with you. Then you tried to sell me just, so you can get high, what the hell is wrong with you. I trusted you Nicole, and this is what you do to people you say you love and care about. Take me home now before I call the police," I was pissed. I was not going to be gullible anymore. "Girl calm down, don't nobody want to hear all that, and hell it ain't like you no virgin anyway, so it doesn't matter who you have sex with now, it will never be anything special. You're used up now babygirl." Nicole said to me as she smoked whatever it was she was smoking. I looked over at Ben with tears in my eyes. Ben grabbed Nicole hands, "You going to take her home now it's already late at night." "What you fell in love with that young cat." Nicole said looking at Ben and then back to me "So I guess your stuff is something special after all." Nicole said and started laughing. "Mia, get your stuff I'm taking you home, and this crackhead is too high to even know what she is saying," Ben told me as he pushed Nicole down on the floor and walked to the door.

"Mia, you can't let what people say get to you especially

if you know it's not true. You know I didn't touch you, so what she said shouldn't matter to you." Ben told me on the way home. "Yeah, but she's right I'm nothing special anymore," I said looking out the window. "So, you going to let a crackhead, someone that's killing themselves every day tell you that you not special, man I thought you were smarter than that," Ben told me shaking his head in disbelief. It was kind of funny because he was the one actually selling her the crack. Ben liked me and he really wanted to protect me. It was something about how innocent and pure I was, but he knew I was too young for him he was eight years older than me and that wasn't a risk he was willing to take.

As we got closer to my house, I could see a couple of cars in front of the house, and I didn't want Ben in any trouble because after all he took care of me for the weekend. He made sure that I was safe even though I was supposed to be given to him. "Drop me off at the corner, and I'll walk to the house. I don't know who's in there and I don't want you to have no parts of what's going to happen." I pointed to the corner where I would get out. "Be safe Mia," Ben told me as I got out of his car and that would be the last time they would ever see each other.

I walked up to the house alone. As soon as I walked in the door, "Mia, where have you been, you think you grown? You just go off for a whole weekend and not tell anybody anything? My mother screamed. She wasn't giving me a chance to say anything. "Mom, Nicole…" before I could finish I was cut off, "Stop lying because I called Nicole and she said she hadn't talked to you in weeks. I don't know what's gotten into you lately, but you are becoming so fast and grown. Where have you been?" I just stood there. It seemed like nothing I would say would make her believe me and I didn't know why. I had never lied to her, so I just didn't understand, I didn't get it, why did she believe everybody else and not her own daughter. Tamara saw the hurt in my eyes and that I was shutting down, and she looked at my mom, "Maybe she's telling the truth maybe this Nicole girl lied to you." Tamara told my mom. "Why would Nicole have lied Tamara, Mia's the one lying. She's just going crazy. I don't know what has gotten into her." My mom said as she walked away, "Just take her to Andre." I finally looked around, and notice that my dad wasn't there it was just my step-mother, my mom, and my step-sister, Sherell who had come down from Chicago. "She probably didn't even tell my daddy what's been going on. Lisa never tells him anything," I said under my breath as I got in the car with Tamara and my sister Sherell.

"Mia, you've never lied to me where were you and what's really going on?" Sherell asked as we rode to Tamara's and my dad's house. "I don't want to stay here anymore, every time I tell my momma something she never believes me so from now on I will never tell her anything ever again in my life," I said as the tears rolled. I was more hurt than angry. This weekend was the second big thing that has happened to me, and I felt as if my mom didn't protect me or even believe me. "So, Mia were you really with this Nicole girl like you said?" Tamara asked me. "Yes, she came and picked me up when I got out of school on Friday. She told me that my mom said it was ok if I went with her for the weekend. She had never lied to me before, so I believed her and got in the car." I explained as we pulled up to the house. "Your dad has been worried sick about you," Tamara said right before the three of us got out of the car. My heart broke because I never even thought about how my dad was feeling or what he would think. When we walked in the house, it was dark, and it seemed like no one was even home. "Mia come here," a voice came from out of the room. I was a little confused because it sounded like my dad, but the voice was a little horse as if this person had been screaming or doing something to lose their voice. When I walked into the room, and I saw my dad sitting in a chair with bloodshot red eyes. I was scared because I had never seen my dad look the way he did.

I sat down on the bed, and for the first time, someone had asked me what I had been waiting for since I got back. "Mia, are you ok?", Sherell asked from the doorway. Everyone just looked up at Sherell. "Hell, no one once asked her was she okay. We don't even know what she has been through this weekend. She could have been raped, beating or anything. All I have heard was everyone pointing the fingers at her and blaming her for something that seems not to be her fault." Sherell said, and she stormed away from the room but quickly returned. "Mia do you want to come stay with me in Chicago?" Everyone just looks at Sherell. "That may be a good idea." my dad finally spoke. "Mia, do you think you need a change. You want to get away and get a fresh start?" He asked me. "Yes, I think I need to moved and get away from here." I quickly answered. It seems like Sherell was the only one that really was concerned with what was going on with me. So, it only made sense to move with the person who has my back.

That night everyone went back to my mom's house where she was waiting. We all sat and talked for hours until everyone all agreed that it was best that I go ahead and move to Chicago with Sherell for a little while. The next morning, I was on the road headed to my new home. I was so excited to be moving to Chicago and starting my life over. Sherell always took me under her wings since daddy and Tamara had been together, so this was nothing new for the two of us. Sherell didn't have kids so I would be the only child in the house. Sherell was married, but her husband was never there he worked over in the island he was from. On the ride to Chicago, I told Sherell everything that had been going on with me. I told her about the demon seeds that snatched away my innocence and how my mom didn't believe me. By the time we made it to Chicago, I had no more secrets that she didn't know about.

We pulled up to one of the biggest houses I had ever seen. "Wow, this is a big house," I said as we walked in the door. "Well this is your house now," Sherell told me pointing to my new room. I was so happy I ran through the house as if I was finally free.

I didn't go back to Miami much once I moved to Chicago. It was just so many bad memories down there, and that's where I wanted them to stay. I didn't speak to my mom that much either because it still hurt and upset me that my mom didn't protect me or even believe me when I finally opened up to her. I loved my mom, but I just didn't want much to do with her at this point. Sherell always told me that once I get older that probably would change. Who knows, guess we will see.

# CHICAGO LIVING

It's been almost four years since I left Miami and moved to Chicago. We stayed near Northside Chicago in a neighborhood called, Lake View. Chicago was so different from what I was used to back in Miami, but I was adjusting well. I had to learn their language because they had their own style up here. I was enrolled in Lake View High School, and I was in the 10th grade. I loved high school and the fact that I was almost on my way to college. I was living the good life, and things were going great for me. I started back speaking to my mom regularly, but still didn't have any plans on going down to Miami. However, she came to visit me a couple of times. Everything was great, but I could never understand how Sherell was able to live this life and she didn't work. I never questioned where or how Sherell was getting her money. I just enjoyed what I was getting and how I was living.

I had a lot of freedom living with Sherell, but overall, I was still a good kid and was able to be trusted with my freedom. I went to school and came home. It didn't take long for the new girl from Miami at the school to become popular. I didn't talk to too many people, but I had become good friends with a girl named Kim. I met Kim when I first moved up here the last two months of middle school. Kim stayed next door, so we did homework together and hung out a lot. I guess she was my Chicago best friend. Chari and Ronyette would tease me about having a new friend, but they were happy for me and knew I wasn't alone up here.

"Hi Mia," Semaj said as Kim and I walked to class that morning. I smiled and waved as I kept walking. "Mia are you just going to wave like the most popular boy in school didn't just speak to you out of all the girls in the school," Kim said as she hit me on the arm. "Girl, if you hit me like that one more time," I said as we stop at our locker we shared. Kim had only been trying to get me to date Semaj since the second week I moved to Chicago. "And you know I speak to everyone he's no different from anybody else." I didn't understand what was so special about Semaj that had all the girls head over heels for him. "Mia, Semaj has liked you forever obviously, and you don't even realize what you got in front of you. And no, I'm not just saying that because he's my cousin." Kim said in disbelief that I didn't care. "Kim, you and him will be alright," I laughed and walked into class. "This girl is crazy," Kim said as she walked in behind me. When I got to my desk, a note was sitting there for me. I opened it as I sat down and read it.

**Mia,**
**Look you are the hottest shorty I've ever seen. I've been trying to get your attention forever now. I think you're raw and I'm trying to be on that with you. But you always dip out before I could get to you and get ya math. Merch, I'm trying to make you my shorty but peeped that I ain't the only G on that. Yeah, I peeped all the Gs talking about how decent you are, and trying to holla at you, but I ain't gone get pressed over it yet. But for real for real you Decent and I ain't cappin. I'm gone make you my shorty no matter what it takes, O.M.S.!**

**Semaj**

I laughed because I finally realize that Kim was right. "What it said, who's that from?" Kim leans over me trying to read the note. "How did he get in here?" I looked at Kim and asked. See I was a year under Semaj, so he shouldn't have been in my English class that day. "How who got in here, girl you are talking about Semaj? I told you he liked you what he say? He asked you for your number, didn't he? So, you going to let him get it or not?" Kim was asking more questions than I could answer. "Kim, girl calm down you're more excited than me." We both started laughing. I thought it was cute, but I still didn't want the attention that would come with being his girlfriend or in the Chicago term, shorty. Besides I had never had a real boyfriend or any type of boyfriend since that little relationship me and Lil Tony had back in middle school.

Later that day while Kim and I are going to lunch someone came from behind and grabbed me. "So, you didn't peep me standing here," Semaj said as he pulled me towards him. I quickly snatched my armed back. "Boy, don't pull me like that and to answer your question no I didn't see you. I wasn't looking for you," I said, this was the first time I actually took a good look at him and notice his eyes were green, he had dimples and the perfect set of white teeth. His body was very built and muscular I guess that came from being an all-around athlete. To say he is fine would be an understatement, and now I could see why all the girls were head over hills for him. I didn't care how fine he was, he had a different girl for every day of the week, and I didn't want any parts of that. "You got my note shorty," Semaj asked, "Yeah I got it," I said unimpressed. "So, you read it or not, and don't cap," Semaj asked me. "I don't have to lie to you," I laughed and walked away. "Shorty, you be tweaking!" Semaj yelled from behind, "Have a better day Semaj." I said as I made sure to make eye contact with him as I kept walking. I guess you can say I was flirting with him, but I didn't have time for him.

After school, I went home and called my two best friends from Miami. "Chari what you doing? Call Ronyette on three-way," I said as Chari answered the phone. "Girl nothing what you been up to up there. You haven't called us in days I guess your new best friend is getting all your attention." Chari said with a little attitude. "Girl don't act like that I've just been busy with all this school work and stuff like that. Chicago is nothing like Miami." They shared a laughed as Ronyette asked, "So how are the boys up there, I heard they fine." I laughed, thinking about Semaj, "I called to tell yall about this dude at school. His name is Semaj, and he's one of the most popular boys at the school, and I guess he likes me. Let me read this note he left on my desk today."

I started reading the note, and immediately Chari stops me after the second sentence, "Mia what the heck is, "be on that with you" mean. Is he trying to have sex already and yall not even dating yet?" Chari asked. I bust out laughing, "No that means like he trying to make me his girlfriend and take me out." I continue reading. "Mia what's get your math, I thought you said he was older than you. Girl, I know you didn't go up there and get you no dummy." "Girl math up here means your phone number." I try to go right back to reading the letter and again was cut off. "Merch, does that mean he going to kill you, oh god do I need to tell your mom to come get you because I can't let my best friend get killed." Ronyette cut in, "Chari shut up so she can finish the letter dang." We all laughed "Chari no one is going to get killed. Merch just means I swear. Let me finish reading the letter girl." I said. "Well, I wouldn't keep stopping you if the people up there would just speak English and words that us normal people could understand.

We laughed, and I finally finish the letter. "Okay I just have one question," Chari said as soon as I finish reading the letter. Rolling my eyes, I answered her question, before she could ask, "Chari fold means to give in, pressed means mad, cappin means lying, anything else Chari." I asked, "Nope you've covered everything for today." Chari said as Ronyette laughed "How did you learn all that talk. Does anybody just talk normally up there?" We laughed and talked for a little while before we all needed to go.

"Mia come eat" Sherell screamed from downstairs in the kitchen. I was shocked she cooked on a Friday. "What you cook?" I asked walking down to the kitchen. "What you been up to Mia?" Sherell asked as she gave me my plate. We both walked to the table to sit down and eat. I sometimes forget she's even married because her husband was always over in the islands where he was born . "Nothing much just going to school and trying to get this year over with," I said as we sat down. "So, who is Semaj?" Sherell asked out the blue. I was caught off guard, "How you know about him? Some boy that like me, but I'm not feeling him like that? He's older than me, plus, he reminds me of the playa type. He can't take a relationship seriously, and I don't have time for drama. You know how I am," I said still looking at Sherell side-eyed. "What you looking at me like that for? What you thought I wasn't going to find out? I told you I know people everywhere up here. And so what he's older than you Mia, it can't be but by one or two years that's not much. For one, you too mature for your age so, maybe you can be that girl that change him and make him take a relationship serious," Sherell said. "Well, I'm not thinking about him or any other boy at this point. I'm just trying to get out of school and go to college and party." I told my sister. "I think you should consider him as your new boo, I hear his daddy got money," Sherell said as she walked away. "My daddy got money too, and I don't want to date nobody just for money," I yelled at Sherell as she walked down the hall leaving me at the table. "Not Semaj daddy money," Sherell yelled back laughing. "What you means not Semaj daddy money? My daddy got money." I said to Sherell, but she just laugh never telling me what that meant.

I couldn't help but think about what Sherell said about Semaj dad having a lot of money. Not that I was any more interested in him because I found out his daddy or whoever had money. I just wanted to know what that meant. I picked up the phone and called the only person who I knew would know all about Semaj and his family. His cousin who just so happened to be my bestfriend. "Hey Mia, what's up chick?" Kim said picking up the phone on the first ring. "Kim, what are you doing?" I asked. "Girl, nothing was just sitting here doing this homework, what you on tonight?" Kim asked. "Nothing, just sitting here," I said laying on my bed. "Come slide then. It's Friday night you don't got nothing to do anyway." Kim told me. "Sherell can I go over to Kim's house for the night," I asked as I started putting on my clothes already knowing Sherell was going to say yeah. "Cool, I'm about to slide out anyway tonight," Sherell said. "Kim I'll be over there in a minute," I hung up the phone.

Sherell and I walked out the door at the same time. I walked next door, and Sherell walked to a Black Bentley that was waiting in front of the house. I never questioned Sherell about who she was going out with or what she was doing. I just knew when I asked Sherell for anything she got it the next day, and that she was safely back home the next day after she went out. I walked into Kim's yard and wasn't too surprised when I saw Semaj sitting on the porch with Kim's older brother Kris. "Hey Kris, is the door open," I said walking up the stairs to the door. "So, my G, you ain't peep me sitting here." Semaj jumped up and opened the door for me. He wasn't used to anybody just giving him the cold shoulder like I was. He's used to having girls doing whatever he wanted when he wanted. "Hey Semaj, how are you," I said with a phony smile. Kris bust out laughing, "Man, Mia you tweaking for real for real." Kris said. "What... I spoke to him, isn't that what he wanted right?" I said walking in the door blowing a playful kiss toward Semaj, "Have a better day, Semaj." Everyone on the porch laughed.

"Merch, I don't know why you on that with Mia when you could get any other girl to be your shorty," Kris told Semaj. "Man cause she decent for real for real. She fresh out here and I'm on that before anybody else try to be on that." Semaj said as he sat back down. "My G, you not folding either I peep," Kris said. Semaj was determined to make me his girl, and he was willing to do whatever it took to get me.

"Kim why you didn't tell me Semaj was over here?" I said bursting into Kim's room. "So, you pressed because the most popular boy in the school which happens to be my favorite cousin is trying to make you his shorty?" Kim asked sarcastically. "Not the point Kim, and I'm not mad at all," I said as I looked in the mirror fixing my hair. "Oh, he caught you lacking," Kim said laughing. "Kim shut up, and no I wasn't expecting to see him." I sat down on the bed. We laughed and talked for a while.

A couple hours passed, and Kris walked into the room "yall hungry we about to get something to eat." "I don't know about Mia, but I'm hungry bring me something back." Kim told her brother. "G, you better get in the whip and come on I ain't bringing nothing back." Kris told Kim as he turned around and walked back to the front door.

"Yall got 2 minutes or we spinnin without yall," Kris said and closed the door behind him. "Mia let's go cause I'm hungry," Kim said pulling me toward the door. "Ok, I'm coming, but I need to go to the house and get my money," I said as we walked out the door. "Naw you good, just come slide I got you," Semaj said as he pulled me to his car and open the door for me to get in.

I never notice until tonight that Semaj was the only kid at the school to have a Mercedes and not just any Mercedes a fully loaded S500, but I wasn't impressed about it though. "G you really putting me in the back for big head Mia," Kris said pushing my head playfully from behind. We laughed and pulled up to a restaurant on North Broadway. "So, what you want to eat Shorty?" Semaj asked me grabbing my hand. For the first time, I didn't pull my hand away, but I got nervous "I'm not really hungry I just want some fries and a shake," I said looking out the window. As Kim and Kris were getting out the car, Semaj pulled out his wallet and handed them a hundred-dollar bill, "G, bring me a #7 with a coke and bring Mia back a large fry and a Strawberry shake. You look like you like strawberry shakes. That's what kind you want, right?" Semaj said looking at me, and I was surprised because strawberry was the only kind of shake I would drink. I just smiled and turned my head, "Yeah I like strawberry milkshakes." I saw Semaj smile from the corner of my eye, "Alright, and get whatever yall want it's my treat since it's because of yall I met my future wife." We all bust out laughing. "Front yo move then," I responded, and they all laughed even harder. "Peep Mia trying to talk like us Chicago people," Kim said as she and Kris closed the door and walked into the restaurant.

Semaj and I sat there for a minute before either one of us said anything. "Semaj what you want from me? You could have any girl at school, hell and probably anywhere else, so why me?" Finally, I asked still looking out the window. I just didn't understand what he thought was so special about me, and would he still feel that way once he found out about what happened to me in my younger years. "You like music shorty?" Semaj asked which confused me. "Yeah, but what does that have to do with what I asked you?" I finally turned around to look at him as he was messing with the radio.

"She's playing hard to get. She's playing, she's playing, but she likes me she likee meeee. I can tell by the look in her eyes that she's into me cause when she passes by and says hi I can tell by her smile...she's playing hard to get, she just won't admit that she likes me she likes me."

Hi-five blasted through the speakers. I couldn't help but laugh turning down the radio, "So, you trying to tell me something with that song." I asked still laughing while Semaj was still playing around with the radio. Not too long after I heard one of my favorite songs playing. "Listen to this song shorty," Semaj said and smiled at me, his smile was so charming.

"I hope that I can make you mine before another man steals your heart and once your beauty is mine I swear we'll never be apart. Walks by me every day her and love are the same the woman has stolen my heart and beauty is her name." Semaj sang to me still holding my hand. Did I mention not only was he fine, but he could really sing too. I didn't picture this happening when I agreed to go over to Kim's house. So, this dude is really singing Beauty by Dru Hill to me, how did he know this was one of my favorite songs. Kim must be telling him this stuff. I cut the radio down, "How did you know I liked this song? Kim must be telling you what I like cause it's funny how you knew I liked strawberry milkshakes when that's the only kind of milkshake I drink." I asked looking at Semaj sideways. "Shorty don't worry about how I know what you like, just know I'm on that," Semaj said with that smile that I found so attractive. "Yeah whatever I know...." Before I could finish what I was going to say, there was a loud knock on the window and cause both us to jump.

"So, this the chick you tweaking on me about. Roll down the window let me see the chick." A girl yelled from outside the driver window. I couldn't help but laughed, "This is exactly why I don't take you serious Semaj, you better rolled the window down before Laila Ali Jr, break it." We both laughed. "You got jokes, man she ain't crazy she just a goofy I use to let give me a kitty boost a couple of months ago, when you wouldn't give me the time of day," Semaj said grabbing my hand tighter. For the first time since we got in the car, I pulled my hand away slowly "Go handle your business playboy, and I'll sit right here, G" they share another laugh before Semaj opens the door to get out. Semaj loved my sense of humor. I was naturally funny without even trying to be. "Let me see the trick, don't get out the car." The girl screams trying to see inside the car as Semaj pushed her away from the car. "G, you are tripping you ain't my shorty, and you never was, we did what we did, and that was that. Stop acting like a lame you knew what it was." I heard Semaj tell the girl through the cracked passenger window I let down just to listen.

Semaj got back in the car, and not too long after Kim and Kris were headed back with the food. "Mia don't snatch your hand away from me again man," Semaj said as he grabbed my hand. I went to pull my hand back, but he grips it a little tighter and the look Semaj gave me was kind of sexy to me, so I just went with the flow and let him be in control this time. I was drawn to the way he always takes charge, and it reminded me of something I would see in the movies. I would never let Semaj know that, not right now anyway. It was something about the chase he was given I liked. "G, I just saw that goofy, Brittney," Kris said as he passes the food out. "Who's Brittney? Oh, never mind that must be Laila Ali Jr." I said, and Semaj bust out laughing. "Yeah, that's who he's talking about," Semaj said passing me my shake and fries. "What did we missed and why you call her Laila Ali Jr., did she try and shoot the one with you?" Kim asked ready to fight. "Kim ain't nobody gone touch Mia, she always protected as long as I got breath in me." Semaj quickly responded to Kim. "Why yall so violent tonight?" I asked looking back and forth between Semaj and Kim. We all just laughed and talked as we rode back to Kim and Kris house.

Everybody started to get out the car, and Semaj grabbed me pulling me back in the car, "Wait until I open the door for you. Act like the queen you are and let me be your King, shorty" Semaj said. I thought it was cute how he was such a gentleman yet had so much hood in him. Even though I was ready to get out the car because I needed to use the bathroom, I waited for him to come around and open the door for me. "Thank you, playboy," I said as I walked to the gate, "Can I open this one or does the King have to open this for me too" I joked, Semaj was falling hard for me in just a matter of hours and I had no idea how hard. He loved my personality, my smile, and my beauty. In his eyes I was perfect. I was nothing like what he was used to. His money, nice clothes, and cars didn't impress me at all. If he wanted me to give him a chanced, it was going to be because of him and nothing more. Semaj opened the gate for me to walk through, "Thanks playboy, but next time can you move a little faster I have to use the bathroom." I said as I pointed to the front door that was already opened from Kim and Kris going inside. "Shorty, you see the door is open," Semaj said, "Well I thought you might have wanted to close it and reopen it. I mean you said I have to wait for you to open every door for me." I smiled and walked passed him blowing him a kiss. "One day you going to be giving me a real kiss watch," Semaj replied as he walked into the house behind me. "And don't be looking at my butt," I knew he was anyway, I caught him doing it a couple of times. "It shouldn't be so perfect," He laughs and closes the door.

"Semaj, you know Mia is not like what you are used to. She, not a goin, she's been through a lot and if that's what you want from her leave my friend along now." Kim told Semaj while I was in the bathroom. "No, she decent for real for real and she raw. You know I've liked her since the first time I saw her, you think she on that with me and don't cap Kim," Semaj asked. "I don't know. She's opening up to you and she hasn't given anybody, especially a dude the time of day since she's moved up here." I walked back in the living room, "What you two talking about, you in here giving him some more tips about what I like and don't like?" I asked sitting down next to Kim on the opposite side of the room from Semaj. "Girl, what are you talking about I never told Semaj anything about you. If he knows anything you better talk to your sister Sherell, not me." Kim said before walking into her room "I'm going to leave you two lovebirds alone for a minute." I shake my head and smile.

"So, you been coming around here talking to my sister about me," I asked as I tried looking at Semaj in the eye. I liked eye contact, but for some reason, I couldn't keep eye contact with him, and I didn't know why. "Mia, I meant what I said earlier tonight," he said as he came to sit next to me. "I know you have to open all the doors for me and I should never snatch my hand away," I imitated him the best I could. "I'm not even your girlfriend so tonight probably was the last time you'll be doing all that." Semaj smile and I quickly looked away. Semaj softly grab my face and turned my head back toward him, so I had no choice but to look into his eyes. "No, when I said you're my future wife and as long as I have breath in me you always going to be protected from anybody." Semaj ran his hand down my face, he didn't know my skin was so soft, and it was turning him on, but he knew he had to take his time with me. Whatever he was thinking wasn't happening no time soon. "Shorty give me a minute let me go holla at Kris."

"Man, listen I think I love shorty," Semaj says as he burst in Kris room. He believed in love at first sight because his dad always told him he'll know when it's real love. "G, man you tweaking you ain't even hit that and from what Kim say she ain't about to let you poke. So how you gone go from a Brittney to Mia, that's a totally different ball game. If you ain't peeped shorty, don't give a damn about your whip or anything you can buy her." Kris said shaking his head. Semaj knew what Kris was saying was true. I was not like any girl from his past, and that's what attracted him to me the most. He knew we were both young, but he wanted to experience the rest of what life had to offer us together. "O.M.S. I'm gone get shorty no matter what it takes and I ain't capin," Semaj sat looking at the ceiling in deep thought. He wanted a relationship like his parents had. They were a real love story. They met when they were kids, had him when they were teenagers, and now they are happily married living as a successful power couple.

Meanwhile, I was still sitting in the living room in my own thoughts. I was catching feelings and having all types of emotions that I had never felt before tonight. After all that I had been through this was the first time someone made me feel good and unique. Yeah, I was used to boys liking me. I mean I had the body most girls only dreamed of having. I was 5'1, 135lbs, small waist, and had curves in all the right places, with long pretty jet-black hair. People always assumed I was older than what I was, because of the way my body was built. I was always told how beautiful I was, I just never felt pretty. But Semaj was making me feel beautiful. I still had my doubts about him. I learned that majority of the dudes that found me attractive only wanted to get between my legs.

"He's crazy he doesn't even know me. How he wants to marry me, besides he'll never take marriage serious he has too many chicks, and we are too young," I found myself saying out loud not knowing that Semaj had walked back in the room. "Well, tell me about you and let me get to know you," Semaj said startling me out of my thoughts. "So that's what we doing, sneaking up on people now." I jumped and pushed Semaj who was standing right behind me. Semaj grabbed my hand and pulled me into him, and we just stared at each other for a couple of seconds. I tried to pull away, but he wasn't letting go. "Shorty, I ain't gone hurt you, O.M.S. And stop worrying about other girls I only want you." Before I could respond, he let me go and walked out the door yelling to Kris, "My G, I'm about to spin." He looked back at me before closing the door, and just like that he was gone.

That night I couldn't stop thinking about what all had happened that entire day. I laid on Kim's room floor while Kim was on the bed. "Shorty, I ain't gone hurt you…" was all that kept playing in my head. Everybody I ever trusted has hurt me, so I can't trust him and believe anything he says, is what I thought. Before moving to Chicago, I promise myself never to get too close to anyone. When I open up to people, they use it against me, and I end up getting hurt. For fear of being hurt I never really took dudes seriously and didn't have a lot of friends. Sherell believes in zodiac signs. She used to tell me it was because I was a Scorpio and we never let people in, because we love hard, but we can hate even harder. So, to keep from hurting anyone we just stayed to ourselves. I didn't know what it was, I just knew I trusted nobody, and the few people I did open up to I still didn't fully believe I could trust them either. But for the first time I wanted to trust Semaj, and the way I was feeling about him I had never felt for anyone.

"Mia girl are you even listening to me," Kim was screaming as she throws a pillow at me. "What you say girl, I was thinking, you know I get lost in my thoughts sometimes," I said throwing the pillow back. "My cousin called you when you were in the shower," Kim said smiling harder than ever. "Why you smiling so hard?" I asked frowning at how happy Kim was and not wanting her to know I was just as happy as her. "Mia can I be honest with you," Kim asked as she sat up in bed. "Kim, you know I only like honesty," I was big on honesty. "I think my cousin really likes you." I couldn't help but laugh because I think I really like her cousin too. "Mia I'm serious, I was standing in the hallway being nosey while yall was talking. The way he looked at you it was different. I never saw him look at anyone like that, O.M.S," Kim told me still smiling. "Girl I can't take Semaj serious, I mean what other 17-year-old boys you know want to be in a serious relationship with just one girl and on top of that talks about marrying so young?" I looked at Kim waiting for her to answer the question. It didn't take long for her responds, "My uncle James married my auntie Sabrina right out of high school right before he went off to college and then went to be a professional football player, all with auntie Sabrina right by his side. Oh, and Rickey also talks about marriage and being with only one girl." Rickey was Kim's boyfriend. "And who is uncle James again?" I asked. "Semaj daddy goofy," Kim said playfully. I forgot that was the real reason I even came to Kim's house that night to find out what Sherell meant by "Semaj daddy money."

We talked a little more about how Kim think Semaj fell in love at first sight and how I need to open up and let my guard down just a little. Finally, she let me go to sleep about 2 hours later. I found out that Semaj was the only child and his dad had played for multiple NFL teams. Which was the main reason I even came to Kim's house in the first place.

# NOT FOLDING

A couple of months had passed since Semaj told me he was going to do whatever it took to make me his shorty when we were at Kim's house. I eventually ended up giving him my phone number. We spent the whole summer talking and meeting up just kicking it. I enjoyed hanging out with Semaj. I noticed when I was with him I always had a smile on my face. But I made sure it was known that we are just friends. Another summer came and gone, and it was the weekend before the start of the new school year. I was riding around with Semaj as he did some last minute shopping. Seems like lately we were always together. Kim started being with Rickey more, so I needed someone to spend my days with. "So shorty you tired of this friendship mess yet and ready to be mine for real for real," Semaj asked as we left Jugrnaut. "No, I like having my options open, just in case it's somebody out there for me." I laughed knowing Semaj was going to get pissed off. Just as I thought he was getting mad, "Yeah, alright, get you and G, wacked," Semaj said laughing. I wasn't worried about him doing anything to me because I always played around with him saying stuff like that. Honestly I wasn't out looking for nobody. I just liked to see him get mad which made him sexier.

We were back in school and the first week flew by. Semaj was a senior, and I was a junior. Football season was in full swing, and I always loved football, so I was at every game with Kim and sometimes Sherell when she didn't have to take care of business. It was gameday Friday at school. Kim and I walked out of class and saw Kris and Semaj standing by the door with their football jersey and jackets on as they usually would every gameday next to the cheerleaders and the band. Semaj called me over to him, so I pulled Kim and walked toward where they were. Brittney was a cheerleader that Semaj was messing around with at one point who just wasn't ready to let go of him just yet. She saw us headed that way, so she decides to make her presence known. She popped up on us while we were out at random places as if she was following us a couple of times. The thing is I didn't care, and I knew that Brittney would always try to be the center of attention, which was the entire opposite of me. Attention seeking wasn't my style at all. "Man, you tweaking," Semaj said as he pushes Brittney to the side and grabs my hand pulling me in front of him. "This chick ain't got nothing on me," Brittney said as she attempted to walk up to me. "Have you looked at her and have you looked at you?" Kris said as he jumped in between us looking at me then back at her. Everybody laughed. "Brittney, G just treated you, just spin while you can." One of their teammates says laughing even harder. "Yeah, he'll be calling me later," Brittney says walking off.

"Shorty you coming to the game tonight?" Semaj pulled me back towards him as I started to walk off. "You know I'm not missing a game for nobody," I told him walking away, blowing him a kiss playfully, "Have a better day

Semaj." That had become our thing. We always flirted, but I still didn't want to be his girl. "Dam, shorty decent for real for real," says Terry, one of the football players, as Willie another player warned him, "Man you better not let Semaj hear you saying anything about shorty." "You better listen to what he telling you, G" Semaj turned around to the two boys that were talking. "O.M.S. I can get shorty math if you stop blocking," Terry said as Semaj was walking off. "You gone be pressed G, when you realize she out of your league," Semaj told his teammate as he turned around before running off to try to catch up with me. Semaj knew I would never give Terry the time of day or so he hoped I wouldn't.

After lunch, we went to get our regular seats that we would sit at for the pep rally. When we arrived at the seats, Semaj had left his jacket in the chair with a note.
Mia

Last night you told me it's starting to be too cold out at the games so wear this. Can't have my good luck charm cold. Have a better day, Mia.

Semaj

I couldn't stop smiling, and I put the jacket on. Everyone started to come into the gym. Terry ran over to me, "Mia you should link up with me tonight after the game to get something to eat." I smiled "Terry you know I am not about to link up with you stop playing." "Man, lowkey Semaj still poking Brittney," Terry told me thinking that would help him win me over, but it didn't go as planned. I didn't like that he was trying to play Semaj just to try to get me. I shrugged my shoulders, "I guess he got to get his rocks off somewhere, cause he ain't poking me, besides I'm not his girl so why are you telling me?" I assured Terry. "Well, who poking you then Mia, cause you too decent to not be letting a G get a kitty boost with you," Terry said moving closer, but stop when Semaj grabbed him. "My G, it definitely won't be you," he said pushing him in the other direction "Semaj, you know I was just bussin with Mia. Besides Mia say she ain't your shorty so why you pressed with me trying to get with shorty?" Terry said backing up, "Mia we gone link up." Semaj turned and looked at me after he heard what Terry said.

I noticed that Semaj would always show up every time I felt uncomfortable or needed him to be there. "So, I see you got my note." Semaj smiled looking me up and down. Right when he was about to ask me about the conversation with Terry, his coach called him. "I gotta spin and get over there with the team, but we gone talk about that not my girl comment later," he said walking away still looking at me, "Shorty that last name looks good on you." "Have a better day Semaj," I told him as he walked off, I blew him a playful kiss, and he turned around and ran over to where the football team was.

"Mia, you might want to look at the back of this jacket, this is not Semaj jacket," Kim said as she was bending back reading the jacket. I took the jacket off and looked at it. I read out loud, "The only Mrs. Davis" and laughed hysterically. I look over at Semaj who I knew was going to be looking he smiled and went on to the court as they announcer called "Our very own all-around star player, our star running back, Semaj Davis." Everyone screamed, and I just continue laughing. "What's so funny Mia?" Kim asked as she sat back down. I finally stop laughing, "Ok so the other night I was talking to Semaj, and I was telling him I needed to get a bigger jacket because it's starting to get cold at nights. He suggested I wear his jacket. Me always joking and playing said the only way I'm wearing his jacket is if I'm the only Mrs. Davis" starting back laughing, I continue,

"So, this fool must've had the jacket made after I said that."
Kim started to shake her head. "You two are so confusing,
either yall friends or yall together." "Kim, we are just
friends for real. You know if it was more than that you
would know." Kim looked at me sideways, "Now you
know you keep secrets better than a locked diary, so don't
try that." We laughed together. "Chicago Bear starting wide
receiver, James Davis is in the building." They heard the
announcer call out. "Look there's uncle James." Kim
pointed toward the middle of the court. I thought I saw
doubles as Semaj and his dad hugged. Semaj was a younger
version of his dad, fine dark tall, and handsome. "Kim why
you didn't tell me he was coming." I elbowed Kim in her
side. "Semaj told me not to tell you because he knew you
would not show up today," Kim said. "Anyway, what's the
big deal you two just friends, right?" Kim teased me,
"Besides Semaj said he asked you to come over and you
told him you're not coming over until you met his parents.
Well, it looks like you be going over tonight if it's up to
Semaj." Kim said as I looked up and saw them walking
over to us. I would've walked off, but they made it over too
fast, and I didn't want to be rude, so I just sat there and
smiled. "Hi Kimmy, how's uncle's favorite niece?" "Uncle
James I'm your only niece," Kim said as they gave each
other a hug, while I was telling Semaj I was going to kill
him behind his dad's back. "Pops, this is Mia, your future
daughter in law," Semaj said pointing to me as I said hi and
laughed. "Hello, Mr. Davis, nice to meet you." "So, you are
the beautiful young lady that's giving Jay a run for his
money, and I see why." Mr. Davis said looking back at
Semaj, "She reminds me of your mom when she was that
age." Looking back at me, "hopefully, you're at the game to
meet her tonight, and I see you got the jacket this boy had
to get made." I smiled feeling a little shy and put on the

spot, "Yes I'll be at the game." Semaj pulled me toward him, "She has no other option if she wants us to win she has to be there. Every player has a good luck charm, mine just happens to be decent." "Mia, what did you do to my son, I've never seen him like this." Mr. Davis said as Semaj and him walked off. "I'll be outside waiting, I'm going to walk pops out," Semaj said. "Hey Mr. Davis," Brittney ran over to them as they were leaving "Hey Brandi, how are you," He said not even looking back. "It's Brittney," she yells trying to get their attention. We laughed as we walked by Brittney. "What the hell you laughing at, he gone poke you and leave you for the next new chick. You, not the first one to get to wear his jacket and won't be the last. He always comes back to me," Brittney said stepping toward me. "So, what you want to pop off(fight)?" Kim tried to jump in between us, but I stopped Kim. I was getting tired of this chick, "See that's the difference between you and me. I poked his mind before he was even able to talk to me on the phone. I never laid on my back for him and he still barking up my tree and worshiping the ground I walk on. I don't get poke period, and when I'm ready to be poke, I'll be poking him not him poking me." I said as I walked off, but I stopped and looked back at Brittney, "And the next time you ever walk up on me you better be ready to pop off. I'm from Miami I don't take too good to people in my personal space." Pointing to her head I continue, "Stop playing with me before you get your feelings hurt. I'm not the one." I said walking off to make sure Brittney was able to read the back of the jacket. No, I wasn't Semaj girl, but I didn't play about people disrespecting me, and this girl had tried me one too many times. I was sweet and a very friendly girl, but the last thing you wanted to do was piss me off and get on my bad side. I had that side to me and once you pulled it out you better be ready for what was to come.

Kim was still in shock as we walked over to Semaj and Kris, "Mia who was that girl about to pop off on Brittney? I never knew you had that side in you. I mean I knew, but that was the first time I saw her come out in a long time" Semaj cut Kim off, "Mia come here shorty," Semaj said pulling me towards him. He was upset, but I didn't know why. I pulled away "Semaj that hurt, what's wrong with you?" "My bad Mia, but what Terry was telling you before I walked up." I looked at Kim because if I tell Semaj what Terry said it wouldn't end nicely for Terry. "So, you know I just got into it with Laila Ali Jr. after you walked out here," I said changing the subject. "Bout what?" Semaj asked looking at Kris. "About you, what else fool," Kim said. "Bout me, for what? That's not my shorty." Semaj said with a nervous laughed. "But you still poking her and Mia knows it, Terry told her today." Kim blurted out. "Kim!!!" I scream slapping her on the arm. "Like I told him and I'll tell you too it doesn't matter to me you gotta get your rocks off somewhere. You not poking me, and I'm not your girl," I said looking at Semaj. He hated when I said I wasn't his girl because that made him feel that at any time someone else could come snatch me away. Before he knew it, he had me pinned to the side of his car standing in front of me so I couldn't go anywhere. "Shorty what I told you about that, stop playing with me for real for real." I calmly asked, "What did I say that was untrue." I knew how to push Semaj buttons and I also knew how to calm him back down. Looking Semaj in his eyes I acted as if I was going to blow him a playful kiss like I always did, but this time I actually gave him a quick kiss. "Yeah.. ok, and ain't no other G gone be on that either," he said moving back and opening the door for me to get in the car. "G, yall be tweaking for real for real. Like why you two don't stop playing this cat and mouse game and just make it official. Mia, you got to fold sooner or later." Kris said as he got in the back seat with Kim. Everybody knew Semaj had a temper, but I was the only one who could calm him down and wasn't afraid of him losing his temper with me. I liked the fact that he was so passionate about me, and I knew he wouldn't do anything to hurt me. "Kim, why did you tell this fool what that boy said, you saw me change the topic, and you went and brought it right back up," I asked Kim while Semaj was walking around to get into the car. "Well, hell you wanted to know if it was true or not," Kim asked as Semaj got in the car. "If what was true?" Semaj asked not missing a beat. "Nothing Jay, let's just go I'm hungry," I told Semaj as we locked hands together. "Yeah, it's true I poked her last night," Semaj said as he pulled off. My heart fell to the floor, I thought I didn't care, but it seems I cared more than I was willing to admit. I was happy he was honest with me. "My G, you tweaking for real for real," Kris said throwing his head back as if he couldn't believe Semaj had just said that. I tried to pull my hand away, but Semaj wouldn't let go, the more I pulled, the tighter his hold got. This was the quietest ride the 4 of us had ever been on. "Mia, what you want to eat," Semaj asked me for the fourth time before I even realize he was talking to me. "I don't care Jay just get whatever," I told him never looking at him. He knew then I was hurt. "Hey Kim, go in there with Kris and order the food," Semaj told Kim handed her some money. "You know the food don't cost this much right," Kim said before getting out the car. He didn't care how much he had given her he just wanted to talk to me alone.

"Mia, you pressed with me?" Semaj asked me rubbing my leg. I just shook my head no. I was never lost for words, but I wasn't the one to let people know how I really was feeling. I was so used to living life as if nothing bothered me, even though I was hurt I wasn't going to let him know. "Mia look at me dam," Semaj told me. "So you want to talk, let's talk" I said turning my entire body all the way around to face him. "So, did you have sex with her before or after you told me you loved me last night," I ask before Semaj could say anything. "I was thinking about you when I was with her." I laughed, "Jay, that's an insult to my pussy and me...I could never be compared to anyone else. So, you thinking about me while poking her will never compare to the real me. Nobody pussy will ever taste or give you satisfaction like mine, but I guess you'll never find that out now will you." I tried to turn back toward the window, but Semaj stopped me, "Mia it won't happen again, I'm sorry." I shrugged "Jay, I'm not your girl we're free to do as we please with who we want to." I was hurt so I decided to take a low blow at him, and that did it. Before I could finish my sentence, Semaj was already opening the passenger door. "Mia stop playing with me for real for real." I laughed "Oh so it's okay for you to actually have sex with someone, but I can't even talk about it hypothetically." "Shorty, who else you been linking up with," Semaj asked me standing in the door. "Jay, are we really doing this right now for real for real?" Semaj was waiting for me to answer him, and I was waiting for him to move. "What these mugs got going on now, Kris?" Kim asked as they were walking back to the car noticing Semaj standing on the passenger side. "Mia said something, and it pissed Jay off I bet. Mia is the only girl I've ever seen him get pressed over." Kris said right before they got to the car. "Let's go Jay, we got a game tonight," Kris told Semaj as they got in the car. "We not moving until she answers my question. Which one of these mugs she been linking up with when I'm not around?" Semaj asked Kim as I laughed.

"What?" Kim and Kris both said at the same time. Everybody who knows Semaj and I could see I was into Semaj. I was just too scared of getting hurt. "Man Jay, you tweaking. You know Mia not linking up with nobody." Kris said as I just looked at Semaj saying, "We can sit here all day long." After sitting there for about 20 minutes and Kris trying to convince Semaj that they are going to be late for the game if they don't leave now, Finally, I said: "Jay I'm not seeing nobody, now let's go before you're late for the game and can't play." Semaj started the car and drove to my house. "Yall be ready by 7, the car will be here to pick you up," Semaj said as he pulled up not looking at me. He was still mad, and I thought it was cute. "Semaj?" I called his name "Yeah Mia." He looked over and realize I wasn't moving until he opened my door. He jumped out the car and ran to open the door. "Thank you, playboy," I said as I walked to the gate. I looked back and yell "Jay you have a better day, and get me 100 yards." He looks at me and smiled blowing me a playful kiss and got into the car and pulled off.

"G you two mugs just blew me. What is it about Mia," Kris said as him and Semaj rode to meet the rest of the team at the stadium. Semaj just laughed, "G, shorty have me tweaking hard for real for real. I'm scared to even poke her at this point. If she got me acting like this now." They both laughed "Kim told me Mia told Brittney that she poked your mind way before you will ever get the chance to poke between her legs." Kris told Semaj. "What G, when this happened." Semaj laughed even harder. "Merch G, Mia told the girl she from Miami and the next time she walks up on her she better be ready to pop off. How the difference between her and Brittney was that she didn't have to lay on her back and she still got you barking up her tree, and some other shit." Kris said trying to act like me.

"Merch," Semaj said still laughing. "But for real for real, Mia raw and Kim says she's been through a lot so if you not serious about her don't play with her," Kris told Semaj as they pulled up to the stadium. "G, Kim keeps saying that but won't ever tell me what she been through. What you know my G, and don't cap either? Semaj said as they walk toward the locker room. "G, ask your shorty I don't know," Kris said and left it at that.

Back at my house, I was sitting on the chair waiting for Kim to finish getting ready so we can go to the game. Sherell had business to take care of so she wasn't going.

"Mia, what the hell was you thinking telling Semaj, you talking to somebody else?" Kim asks as she was putting on her clothes. I laughed, "that's not what I said he just took it that way." Kim walked over to me, "Why are you so scared to let this dude love you Mia, you have to start trusting someone." "So, what's up with you and Rickey?" I quickly change the subject as I often did when it was a topic I didn't want to talk about which was mostly about myself. "Girl we gone link up after the game tonight because I'm sure you going to leave me for your boo thang, I meant friend," Kim said playfully.

We made it to the game right before the team came out. "Thank God, cause this fool would've had a fit if I was a minute late," I said as we sat down the team ran out and the crowd went crazy. Semaj looked up at the stand right behind their sideline where I always sat since my freshman year, we locked eyes, and Semaj smiled nodding his head as I blew him a kiss, and then he quickly looks at the other side. "Oh, look there's Uncle James and Auntie Sabrina. Let's go say hi." Kim tried pulling me up, but I pulled back "Let's not go say hi." Causing Kim to sit back down. "Damn you really strong for a girl." We both laughed.

It was halftime, and Semaj had already run for 100 yards

and 2 touchdowns. The team was preparing to go to the locker room. Kim and I were getting ready to go to the bathroom and get something to drink. "It wasn't as cold as I thought it was going to be so I didn't have the jacket on instead I was carrying it on my arm. I walk by the team "Shorty where you going?" Semaj ran over to the gate real quick. "to the bathroom," I stop to talk to Semaj for a second. While talking a group of boys from the other school walked by, and one said "Shorty decent for real for real," while he tried grabbing my waist. I moved away as quick as I could. I didn't want Semaj to think I knew this dude or anything especially after what happen before the game. I was used to boys hitting on me, but no one had ever tried it in front of Semaj. "Jay, I change my mind I'm going to sit back down I'll wait to after the game." I was trying to get Semaj attention off the dude and back to me. It didn't work, "G, what you on," Semaj yelled at the group of dudes. The group came back, and once they saw Semaj, they quickly change their approach. "G, Merch I ain't peep shorty talking to you, Semaj," Dude said and then walked away. "Jay focus on what you came to do." I said pointing up to where the scouts were sitting, "You got people watching you so give them a show." Semaj smiled and ran to the locker room after the team.

I turned to go back and sit down, but was face to face with Mr. and Mrs. Davis, "Well hello pretty lady you are one beautiful girl." Mrs. Davis said as she smiled and offered me a hug. "Thank you, and you are beautiful yourself," I said as I embraced Mrs. Davis. I wasn't just saying that to be nice either. Mrs. Davis was beautiful and could go for Semaj sister instead of his mom. If she was a little taller you would have thought she was a model. "Mia, thank you for keeping Jay, focus just now. That's what Sabrina used to do on my game night, and she still does, now that I think about it." Mr. Davis said smiling at his wife as if they were still high school sweethearts. I had never seen a man look at his wife the way Mr. Davis looked at Mrs. Davis. It reminded me of how Semaj would look at me. "Well, we hope to see you Sunday for Semaj's birthday dinner." Mrs. Davis said as they walked back to their seats. I just smiled, I had no plans of going to dinner with them. I wasn't going to tell them that though.

Halftime was over, and it was starting to get chilly, so I put my jacket on as Semaj, and the team was running back to the sideline. "The Only Mrs. Davis, turn around and cheer for ya boy," Semaj yelled right before he went back on the field. I turned around and blew him a kiss as I did at every start of the half. By the fourth quarter, Semaj had another 100 yards and 3 more touchdowns. He scored 5 out of 6 touchdowns the team had. After the game Kim and I were walking toward where the players would exit the locker room. "Hey, Uncle James and Auntie!" Kim screamed with excitement when we made it to the locker room. They all stood there and talked and not long the players came out. Semaj walked out and spotted us standing to the side. He started to walk in our direction, but before he could make it to us, Brittney stops him, "So you gone come slide tonight or what?" She said it loud enough to make sure I could hear her. Everyone eyes were on me, and I quickly looked the other way. I knew they would all be looking at me to see what I would do. It was a typical Brittney move, she was always doing stuff like this, but when I acted as if I didn't see what was going on Kim said, "this trick just ain't gone stop til Mia pop off on her." I couldn't help but turn around now. "Kim, it's nothing. I'm cool, that's Semaj's problem to handle not mine." I said as I started to walk over to where Semaj was. "Hey, let me get the keys to the car it's cold out here." I held my hand out as

Semaj looked for his keys. "Girl, he doesn't let nobody hold the keys to his…." Before Brittney could finish Semaj handed me the keys. I looked at Brittney smiled and walked off, "Don't take too long Jay. Handle your business playboy," I patted Semaj on the chest walking off never looking back. I left Semaj and Brittney standing right there never breaking a sweat. I wanted her to know nothing she did or try to do would change the feelings Semaj had for me, and whatever relationship Brittney thought they used to have couldn't even compare to me and Semaj friendship, so imagine if I did become his girl. "So that's what we do now you letting other tricks drive your whip, and I couldn't even hold the keys to your whip. I could barely ride in it." Brittney sounded embarrass and hurt. I didn't feel no sympathy for her at all. "I told her to stop playing with me, or she was gone get her feelings hurt," I mumble to myself walking back over to Kim and Semaj's parents. "Mia, we going to the car." I looked at Kim and laughed, "No, I just felt I needed to show her, stop playing with me before you get your feelings hurt." Kim and I laughed and then heard Mrs. Davis laughing "James, I think I love this girl she's a mini-me all over again." Mrs. Davis told us a similar story about when she was in high school, and a girl was doing the same thing as Brittney. We all shared a laughed as Semaj finally made his way over to where we were, while Brittney watches from behind him. "It took you long enough," I had a little attitude "Shorty, I thought you were headed to the car." Semaj looked over to his mom and dad "what's up pops, hey momma. I see you met Mia?" Semaj gave his mom a hug and a kiss. I could tell that Semaj loved his mom and had a lot of respect for her just by looking at him talk to her. "Yes, I did I was just telling your dad, that I think I love her already." We begin walking to the car, "Good, cause I do too," Semaj said pulling me to keep walking as we all headed to the parking lot. I looked over at Kim shocked. Semaj had never actually told me he loved me in front of other people and I wasn't expecting him to say it right then either. "I told you," Kim whispered. "Well, it was nice meeting you Mia, and we'll see you Sunday for dinner." Mrs. Davis said as Mr. Davis opened the door so she could get in the car. Now I see where he gets his gentlemen ways from. "Alright son, don't get into no trouble and let me know how she likes it. Be safe, you too Kris." Mr. Davis pointed as he pulled off. "Like what," I asked confused. "Alright yall, I'm gone," Kim said as she saw Rickey motioning for her to come over. "Well you two on yall on tonight. I'm trying to get a kitty boost tonight," Kris said as he ran off and jumped in a car with some random girl.

"So, what time you going to poke Laila Ali Jr.," I said as I got in the car. Semaj just shook his head, "Shorty you tweaking for real for real." "Jay listen if you want to be with Brittney go ahead. I'm good for real." I said as we started driving off. Before I knew it Semaj was slamming on the breaks, "Mia stop playing with me, I told you I'm not messing with that chick no more." I laughed, "You was surely talking to her a long time just now, and you were just with her last night," I looked at him, "your words not mine." "Either you want to be with me, or you don't. You say you don't but your action say otherwise," Semaj said as he rubbed my leg. It was something about the way he touched me it cause my body to become hot instantly. "Jay stop," I tried to move. Semaj put the car in park and leaned over to me as if he was about to kiss me, I didn't know what was about to happen, and for the first time, I wasn't in control. He stops right before his lips fully touch mine, "Mia, you love me  and want me stop fighting it." And just like that, we were driving again. Semaj turned the radio on

♪

and through the speakers Keith Sweats starts to sing, **"Mmm Ooohh….MY, my, my, my, my, my baby. You're mine, mine, mine, mine. I'm gonna love you, right girl! You may be young but you ready. Ready to learn…. Take my hand let me tell you baby"** Semaj held his hand out as he usually did and I place my hand in his. As Keith Sweats voice continues to sing everything Semaj wanted to say to me. "Don't take my love for granted you're all I, I'll ever need." The music went mute long enough for Semaj to ask me "Do you trust me?" I didn't know how to answer the question because I wanted to trust him, but I was afraid. My pass was messing with my future and probably happiness too. "Do you trust me to keep you safe and to protect you Shorty?" Semaj changes the question. That was easier for me to answer, "Yes," I answered without hesitation. "Ok, that's all I need to know you going with me tonight," Semaj said right before he turned the music back up, and let Keith Sweat keep singing, **"There's a right and a wrong way to love somebody…A right way to love somebody, you love me right."** I listen to every word of Keith Sweat hit song Right and Wrong Way like I had never heard the song before. We had been driving for about 30 minutes, and we finally pulled up to what looked like a hotel, but it could be a condo. I wasn't sure what it was. We were by the beach so it could be either one. "Jay, I know you didn't bring me to no hotel." I looked at him as if he was crazy. "Shorty, coolin you mean more to me than to just take you to a hotel. Besides, why would I pay money for a hotel when I know you ain't letting me poke nothing." Semaj laughs as two valet guys walked over to both sides of the car to get us out. "Hello, Mr. Davis, welcome home." The doorman said as he opened the door.

I was confused because I knew that Semaj had a house, not a condo. "Jay where are we at," I said as we walked into a condo overlooking the North Avenue Beach. "This is my house, well our house. It was an early birthday gift from my pops. This is what he meant by let him know if you like it," I walked over to the floor to ceiling window and looked at the water as the lights shine on it. "I can't live with you, but this is beautiful." I said as Semaj walked up behind me. "I'm going to ask you again, do you trust me?" I turned to look Semaj in the eyes, "I can't afford to get hurt again in my life." I quickly turned back to look out the window. "Mia, you didn't answer me," Semaj turned me back toward him. I couldn't look at him for some reason. I didn't want to say the wrong thing. My heart wanted to say yes I trust you, but my mind was saying no, so I said nothing at all. Semaj had learned me, so he let it go. "Mia go take a shower I have a surprise for you," Semaj told me pointing to the bathroom. "I don't have any clothes here, what am I going to put on?" I walked behind Semaj, and he walked me around the condo. "Nothing," Semaj laughed, "I'm joking, you got plenty of clothes, shoes, panties, bras, whatever you need you got it here already. "What about pads?" I smile before going in the bathroom and locking the door. "Your period ain't on, but yeah I got them for you too, smartass," Semaj yelled through the locked door. "How you know when my period is on or not," I yelled as I looked in the closet full of clothes I assumed was for me. I notice a black teddy dress laid out with matching panties. "I told you I know all that you allow me to know, and more I'm just waiting for you to tell me," Semaj said as he set up for my surprise.

I stood in the bathroom for a minute I was in a condo that could be mine, with a boy that could be the love of my life 2 weeks shy of my 17th birthday. "Am I dreaming, how did I even end up here. I went from living a nightmare every weekend to living in a fairytale love story. Am I ready for this?" I say to myself as I look in a mirror before stepping into a nice warm shower. While in the shower I decide to trust Semaj and that I deserve to be treated like the Queen I started to believe I was. "Ok, I'll go with the flow for once," I told myself as I got dress and put on the robe. Taking a deep breath, I walked out the bathroom thinking I was ready to finally trust someone. No one had ever seen my body since I had moved to Chicago over 4 years ago, and a lot had changed in those 4 years. I was half naked about to walk out to a room that the man who worship the ground I walked on was waiting for me in. I walked out to Semaj setting up a massage table. "Jay, what are you doing?" I asked as I walked past him and back over to the window. I was nervous and unsure of what was about to happen. Semaj looked up and saw the back of me, "Damn..." Semaj said before he knew it. "Well, I hope that's a good Damn," I continue to look out the window. It's funny how everybody thought I was this fine girl, but I was still insecure about my body. I was just starting to believe I was beautiful, no matter how many people would tell me that I was fine and pretty, it didn't matter until I started to believe it. "Shorty, you might need to go change for real for real. I wasn't expecting you to look that damn decent. No, keep that on matter of fact." Semaj finish setting up the massage table.

"Come sit down let's talk," Semaj said as he sat on the sofa. I went and sat down beside him, and that was the first time Semaj saw me from the front. He took a couple of deep breaths before he took my leg and pulled it up to him. "Jay, what you doing?" I asked nervously. "Just chill, I'm just going to rub your feet you been up on them cheering me on all night that's the least I could do. Didn't you say you trusted me to keep you safe and to protect you." Semaj started rubbing lotion on my lower leg and foot. "Yeah," I said as I began to eat the fruit that Semaj had set up on the table. "Ok so if I'm here to protect you I can't hurt you, if I did I wouldn't be doing my job." I never looked at it that way, but it made sense. We talked as Semaj massage my legs and feet. Semaj picked me up carrying me over to the massage table. "Shorty take that robe off and lay on your stomach. I hesitated at first, and looked over at Semaj, "Trust." was the only word that he said as he throws his hands up in the air. I untied the robe and let it drop to the floor. I stood there for a second as Semaj looked me up and down. He then help me up on the table and I laid on my stomach. Jesus, what am I about to get myself into? Semaj thought to himself. He placed a sheet over me to cover my lower body, just so he wouldn't get distracted from all my ass that this teddy barely was covering, and be tempted to touch places he shouldn't be focus on. He was already tempted when I was fully clothes, so he knew if he didn't cover me up this night was going to go in a whole different direction that I wasn't ready for. Semaj pull the straps on the teddy off of my shoulders and begin to rub and massage my shoulders and neck. The touch of his hand cause me to exhale without even realizing I did it. "Relax Mia you tightening up I told you I'm not going to hurt you, and I am not going to make you do anything you not ready for." Semaj moved down to the middle of my back, as I tried to relax more. Music started to play. We communicated through music a lot when we didn't want to say much, but had something to say to one another. So I wasn't surprise when another one of my favorite songs came on.

**"Emotions makes you cry sometimes, Emotions make you sad sometimes, emotions make you glad sometimes,**

but most of all it makes you fall in love"

We both song with the music. "Get up come dance with me" Semaj helped me up. I put the robe back on, but didn't tie it this time. I took Semaj's hand, and he pulled me into him. We started to slow dance to the music which was a first for me. Semaj started to sing to me while we dance.

**"And when I turned 13, first time I had a freaky dream yeahh..now that I'm 19 I know that I'm ready, I know that I'm so in love yeah soooo in loveeee yeah yeahh.."**

Semaj gently grab my chin to make sure I didn't turn my head from looking in his eyes as he continues to serenade me,

**"See you may go through emotions sometimes and even have some ups and downs, but I know one thing for sure you're gonna fall in loveee. Make you fall in love."**

He let my face go, as I laid my head on his chest. Not only was he handsome and charming, but his voice when he song would make any girl fall in love.

"Mia, when you going to stop playing this game and let me take care of you and be that G you need," Semaj asked me as the music continue to play. "You got me," I didn't even realize I allowed myself to finally give in. After almost a year of him chasing and trying to get me to say the words, he finally heard them. "I told you I wasn't gone fold, shorty." Semaj kiss my forehead. He carried me to the bedroom as he laid me on my stomach and started massaging my lower back, this time he didn't cover my butt, and I didn't make him either. He pulled my dress up, and I jump, "Relax Shorty, I got you on my soul." I felt his hand grab my butt and begin to massage it. I started to get hot, and my heart started racing again, but this time I didn't fight it I just allowed my body to accept what was being done. Semaj slowly moved down to my upper inner thigh, and as soon as he started rubbing, I became moist between my legs, something I had never experience. Semaj didn't stay in the area too long because he didn't want his hands to slip too far to the middle. He leans over to my ear and whispers "Admit you love me shorty," as he gently bit my ear. "You already know the answer to that." I turned to look at him. "I know, but I want you to tell me," Semaj said. I couldn't say it, those words would open me up to be hurt. I looked away instead. Semaj lays on top of me making sure I could feel what he was working with, then jumped up and kiss my forehead, "Don't worry you will say it sooner than you think." Semaj walked to the bedroom door to head to the guest room. I turned to look at him, and he was looking back at me smiling, "So who's poking who's mind now?" Semaj closed the door leaving me thinking about what just happen. First thing I did was feel between my legs, and I realize where the moistness was coming from. So this is what they mean when they say hot and bothered, I thought to myself as I lay there trying to calm down. This was the first time I ever wanted a man to touch me. I was happy that Semaj didn't try to have sex but confused as to why he didn't. I thought that was his reason for wanting me so bad. For Semaj to be young he definitely knows how to treat me. He makes me feel like I'm the only person that matters.

In the guest room, Semaj had just got out the shower and was talking to Kris on the phone. He had to call somebody to keep his mind off the half-naked girl he was in love with in the other room. "G, it's taking all the power in me not to go back in there." Semaj laid on the bed as he talks to Kris. "My G you tweaking, Mia too decent to not poke that ass." Kris laughed at Semaj. "I can't, Mia's different... I have to take my time with her, or else I'll lose her. I got to get her to trust me so I can figure out what she's hiding from me. I've asked Kim she won't tell me, and I even asked Sherell, and she wouldn't tell me either." Semaj and Kris talk for a little while longer before getting off the phone. As bad as Semaj wanted to come make love to me all night long he knew he couldn't, but the way my body was feeling he might have got his chance tonight. He rolled over and looked at the picture of us he had framed. "I'm going to make you love me," Semaj said to the picture before he went to sleep.

The next morning Semaj woke up to the smell of food being cook. "So now you a chef, shorty." Semaj walked up behind me. "If you think you love me now, wait until you taste my food," I said handing him a plate of pancakes, eggs, and bacon. "See this is real southern cooking, not that mess you used to eating." I sat down and joined Semaj at the table. I looked at Semaj sitting across from me and thought to myself, how did I become so lucky at such a young age. "Shorty, what you on?" Semaj notices me staring at him. "Just thinking why you pick me when you could have had anybody." I walked over to the refrigerator. "Why not you, Mia? Besides, the bible said he who finds a wife finds a good thing or something like that." Semaj never looked up from his food, and I laughed at him trying to quote scripture. "How you learn to cook like this for real for real?" Finishing up his food as I took his plate. "I have been cooking since I was a baby don't play with me," I joked. "Shorty, for real for real why you don't think you deserve love." Semaj walked pass me to sit on the sofa. "Everybody I ever love wasn't there when I needed them," I look Semaj in his eyes. He could see the pain in my eyes when I said those words, and he didn't like it, but he was just as surprise as me because I was starting to open up to him. "Shorty, you good OMS, just keep being you and you can have the world. I ain't been chasing you for almost a year to hurt you." I wanted to trust him, and I was open to loving him, but was I really going to be able to give him all my trust? "Go get dress I'm taking you out for the day," Semaj headed to the bathroom to take a shower and get dress.

I called Sherell to let her know I was ok. "So, did you officially give your virginity away by choice last night?" Sherell says without a hello, which caught me off guard. "What? Sherell this is Mia." I thought, maybe she thought it was somebody else. "Girl, I know who this is, now answer my question," Sherell laughed. "Well hello to you too, I am fine and to answer your question no I didn't give my cat to anyone last night or any other night." We laughed. "And how you knew I was even with Semaj?" I asked looking in my new closet for something to wear. "I'm closer to his family then you know, and we'll talk about that later. Anyway, so how do you like your new house Semaj brought you? I told you Andre didn't have Semaj daddy money," Sherell laughed and teased me. "This is not my house, I'm too young to live with a boy." I finally found something to put on. "Girl I moved out at 16 and been on my own ever since. Your age says you're only going on 17 but your mind and body says you are at least 25." Sherell always told me that. "Well I will think about it, but as for now I still stay with you." "Mia don't mess this up for yourself still thinking about what you have been through. Semaj is a great kid and has a great future ahead of him. Do you know how many females would love to take your place? Stop fighting what was meant to be." Sherell ended the conversation.

# NO MORE SECRETS

Semaj and I left the house and instead of going to get the car. Semaj took me, and we walked on the side of the building. I notice rose petals on the floor as we walked toward the beach that I had been admiring last night from the window. Semaj was always doing something to make me feel special. Before we made it to the gate that took us to the sandy beach Semaj stops and turned to me, "You trust me, right?" I start to get nervous because he was asking me that a little too much lately. "Should I not trust you? Should I be scared?" I laughed nervously, "Just don't push me in the water because it's cold and I don't want to mess my hair up." Pulling a blindfold out his pocket and putting it around my eyes, "Shorty, you tweaking ain't nobody gone mess up your hair, at least not in the water." He ties the blindfold tight. "Besides I'm the one who pays to get your hair done." We started to walk, "Wait, take off my shoes I have on heels, and I don't want sand to get in them." I was starting to let my guard down minute by

86

minute. If it were anybody else this probably wouldn't be happening, I always had to be in control. "Man...you would go pick the most expensive shoes to put on today out of all days." Semaj notice I had on a pair of Gucci heels he had brought me. I shrugged I didn't know how much they wear I just liked wearing heels, and those were the ones that match my jeans. "Well, if you didn't want me to wear them you shouldn't have brought them. Besides you said we were going out not to the beach next time tell me a location so I could dress accordingly." I took Semaj hand and allowed him to lead, and I followed. "Shorty, I see you finally allowing me to lead you." "Well do I really have a choice I can't see for myself." My feet sink into the sand, so I knew we were on the beach, but I didn't know for what. Suddenly I could hear the water getting closer and closer. I stop walking, and Semaj pulled me, but I wasn't moving without a fight, "Jay, I'm not playing with you don't throw me in the water for real." Semaj bust out laughing, "Man, come on!" He pulled, and I had no choice but to move he was just stronger and bigger than me. We stop, and Semaj sat me down still blindfolded he sat behind me and place his head on my shoulder, "Mia what's your biggest fear?" I never really thought about fears too much. The only thing I always thought about was the fear of being hurt. "I don't know, what's yours?" I sat wondering how long he was going to leave this blindfold on. "Hurting the people, I love. Not being able to make sure they are taking care of and…. losing you." Semaj untied the blindfold. I looked around and saw rose petals and candles all around us. It looks like something you would see in a movie. "Semaj, how are you so romantic, but so hood," I laughed looking around. "Shorty, wait a minute now. I don't do this for every girl I know. Everybody don't get this treatment, you just special, and I want you to know how you should always be treated." Semaj said feeding me a chocolate cover strawberry. "Besides I peeped my pops treat my O.G. like a queen my whole life. So, I know what you deserve...you just don't know what you deserve, but you'll get used to it." I laid back on Semaj and just watch the water. A couple minutes went by before Semaj said, "Mia let's have a baby?" I jumped up, "What? I'm too young for a baby dude. I have to finish school and go to college." I sat back down, "Besides you go off to college this summer... who's to say you won't find someone there and decide that you're in love with her and start a family with her and forget all about me." Semaj jumped up, and I knew he was pissed, but I was just saying how I felt. He walked off toward the water and stood there for a couple of minutes. He'll be alright I thought to myself and laid back on the beach chair looking at the water as I waited. Finally, he walked back over to me, picking me up like I didn't weight 135lbs. It was easy for Semaj to lift me up with no problem he was 6'2 235lbs of pure muscle. Anybody else would have been in fear of what Semaj was going to do, but it actually turned me on. I wrap my legs around his waist as he cuffed my butt in his hands, and he just walked carrying me without saying a word. Finally, he stop walking when we came to a blanket with a picnic basket sitting on it. "Shorty, stop trying to make me pressed by saying goofy stuff," Semaj said as he sat down still holding me. "My pops and O.G. met when they were kids and started going out in 7th and 9th grade. They fell in love, and my O.G. had me when she was 15-years-old. She finished high school went to college and is now the best sports attorney in Chicago. So, don't tell me about you're too young. I was made off young love." Semaj said standing up still holding me and then finally putting me down. "I'm sorry I have never seen a real love story in real life. That only happens in books and movies for me. Everybody I know ended up raising the baby along and then they marry somebody new who has kids....then the step-kids end up molesting your daughter." I caught myself, "Dam" I mumble. "What you said Shorty?" Semaj asked and I looked at him, "Semaj, I was just giving an example of what could happen." I tried my best to cover up the truth. "Mia, stop playing with me what did that mean?" Semaj grabbed my face because I wouldn't look at him, and he saw my eyes full of tears he let me go because he knew the answer just by looking in my eyes. I looked at Semaj, and I saw a rage in him I had never seen, and for the first time, I was afraid not for me, but for whoever he was thinking about hurting. "When did it happen Mia and for how long?" Semaj looked over at me, and for the first time, he couldn't protect me from my past, as the tears rolled down my face. "Are we really doing this right now Jay?" I looked over at him pleading "Please, don't do this right now Semaj. I can't..." Semaj grabbed me and just held me as I begin to cried like he had never seen me cry. I never showed my emotions or that anything affected me. So, he knew something bad had to happen and he didn't like it. "I'll take care of this OMS. Merch, I got you." We sat there for a little while before we decided to go back upstairs.

As we walked back up to the condo, Semaj called Kim. "Shorty, Kim gone come slide. I gotta spin real quick." Semaj told me as I took a shower. He stood there and watch me for a minute before I notice. "Jay, get out!" I screamed playfully. "Hell, you belong to me, I can see what's mine. With ya decent ass. I'm one lucky G, for real for real," he walked out the bathroom and picked up the phone, "Uncle Steve I need to holla at Sherell now," Semaj knew that Sherell and his uncle had been messing around for years. He would go to Sherell to find out everything he wanted to know about me and Sherell would tell him. Sherell felt like after all, I had been through I deserve someone to take care of me. Semaj being in love with me was a bonus in Sherell's eyes. "She's in the room, come holla at her." Semaj grabbed his keys and left. "I'mma slide now." Semaj was out the door before I even got out the shower.

When I got out the shower, Kim was already there sitting in the living room. Kim looked at me, and my eyes were puffy like I had been crying for hours, because I was.

"Mia what's wrong, I thought you would be happy. Jay, actually went out and got you a condo. How many other girls our age could get a nigga to go out and buy them a condo? I went with Semaj and picked everything out for you." Kim didn't know why I was so upset. "I do love everything about the condo, and I should've known you had something to do with it, you know how much I love the ocean view." I gave a half smile as I sat on the sofa beside Kim. "So, why it looks like you been crying all day and why was Semaj so mad when he told me to come over here." Kim started fixing my hair. "I told Jay…well, I kind of told Jay." I laid on Kim's lap, and she immediately knew what I was talking about. It was only one secret that I never talked about, and that was my past. "Mia, how did you kind of tell him?" Kim was still rubbing my head. "Well we were talking about kids, and I said I was too young…" Kim cut me off. "Wait did you let Jay poke, or yall even official now?" Kim got excited. "Kim no I didn't let him poke, and yes I finally told him I would be his girl. Anyway, so I went to tell him I was too young to have a baby and that he may go off to college and find him somebody and leave me with a baby, then my baby may end up with a stepdaddy who has kids and those kids may come and molest my baby. He put two and two together and figured it out." I begin to cry again. I would always blame myself for what took place. "Mia don't cry you have to stop feeling like you cause this to yourself." Kim says as she wiped my tears. "Yeah, but now will he still think I'm special? Would he still want to be with me?" I asked looking up at Kim. Kim quickly thought about Semaj, "Mia where did Semaj say he was going?' Kim sounded concerned. "He didn't say he left when I was in the shower, I heard him say something about Uncle Steve, but I didn't really hear what he was saying. "Semaj is going to kill them, Mia." I sat up, "Semaj is going to kill who?" I asked looking at Kim, "he's not going to kill nobody… he doesn't even know who it was." Kim shook her head, "Mia, Uncle Steve is Sherell's boyfriend. Sherell has been telling Semaj everything he knows about you. The music you like your favorite color anything he asked her she told him because she wanted you to be with someone who would give you the world. Semaj has liked you since you moved up here, when I came over to meet you it was because he asked me to." I know Sherell wouldn't tell him this, "Well, she isn't going to tell him who did it," I hoped she wouldn't, "she knows not to tell anybody without talking to me about it first." Kim got up and walk to the kitchen, "Hopefully you're right because if not this is going to be really bad."

Semaj pulled up to his Uncle Steve's house and walked in, "Sherell I need to talk to you." He was still upset about what he partially found out. "Nephew what got you so pressed, G." Uncle Steve walked from around the corner. "Hold on nephew, last time I saw you like this I had to pay all type of attorney fees and fines to keep you out of jail for assault and battery charges." Uncle Steve laughed and they walked toward the room Sherell was in. "So, for you to be this pressed Mia must have told you the real reason she moved away from Miami." Sherell sat up on the bed. "Sherell tell me what happen to Shorty. She kind of told me, but she didn't tell me." Semaj sat on the floor. "Semaj, I can't talk to you about that... me and my sister have always kept each other secret, and I can't betray her in that way. She already doesn't trust anybody, but me so if I tell you that, she will never trust anybody again." Sherell felt sorry for Semaj because she could tell he really wants to know so he could help Mia. "Sherell I need to know what happened?" Semaj pleaded with Sherell. "What did Mia tell you?" Semaj began to tell Sherell what happened and how they got to him sitting on the floor in front of her asking her about the secret, so few knew about. "Shorty, don't even know I'm here talking to you." Semaj stood up and looked out the window. "Semaj, Mia was sexually assaulted as a little girl by her mother's husband two sons. After she finally was comfortable with opening up to people, she told her godsister, Mia didn't know that the girl started using drugs... she basically kidnapped Mia and tried to sell Mia to her drug dealers. So that's the reason Mia doesn't trust anybody or let anyone get close to her. She doesn't want to open up to people." Semaj turned around to look at Sherell, "What kind of sick.... How long did they touch her?" The look in Semaj eyes was pure rage. "I've already told you too much. My sister is going to kill me." Sherell shook her head no. "Uncle Steve, they the opps and I want they head!" Semaj walked out the door without anyone even realizing he was gone.

Before arriving back to the condo, he went and got some roses. I loved roses, so he brought 3 dozen roses. A red dozen, a white dozen, and a lavender dozen. Kim had left over an hour ago, so I was there alone when Semaj arrived back. "Jay where you been? I've been calling your cell phone all day and you not once answered me." I was laying on the sofa watching tv. "I cooked you something to eat, but I'm sure it's cold now. I'll warm it up." Walking into the kitchen to warm up the food. "Look, Mia, I thought these would make you feel better after earlier," Semaj handed me the roses and for the first time he saw my eyes were puffy and red. "Mia…" Knowing he was going to ask me about them, I did what I do best change the subject "I cooked rice, corn, chicken, and cornbread. The roses are beautiful. You have to get a vase to put them in so we could put them on the dining table." "Look under the counter, you think I wouldn't have a vase as much as I buy you roses." He smiled. As I take the food over to the table where Semaj was sitting I ask him, "Do you know the meaning for each of these color roses or did you just picked them?" Placing the plate on the table, Semaj pulls me down to sit on his lap. "For you the red means love and beauty, the white means pure and innocence, Lavender means love at first sight." I was impressed. I smiled and looked at the roses as I put them in a vase. "Shorty, how long did it go on?" Semaj asked in the most sincere voice I had ever heard. I face Semaj, "Semaj that was a long time ago. It doesn't matter. Where have you been all day?" I asked Semaj. Sherell called right after Semaj had left to tell me what she had told him, when he came to see her, so I knew he had gone over there to talk to her. I needed to know if I could trust Semaj as much as he wanted me to. "I went to talk to Sherell," he said as he started to eat. I was relieved he told the truth because our future was riding on what he said. "What do you want to know, Jay? I'll tell you myself." I tried to get up but was being held down. "Just tell me how long they did it I already know who did it, but Sherell wouldn't tell me how long or any of the details." I took a long deep breath and closed my eyes "It started when I was seven. It started off with just one and then both of them." Semaj was glad my eyes were closed because he was getting emotional. "How long Mia? How long did this happen to you?" "4 years" I still had my eyes closed. "Did they poke you, Mia?" Semaj let the tears roll down his face. He had never cried for any girl before this. I guess that's because he had never loved any girl before me. "Semaj, that's not important." "Mia, did they poke you?" Semaj voice was full of anger. "He tried…" I open my eyes to look at Semaj. When I saw him with tears in his eyes, I knew that he really did care about me and wasn't just talking. I wipe his tears and smile at him, "I'm okay now Jay for real. This doesn't change anything we have…Does it?" I was scared that now he knew my secret I wouldn't be worth the wait for him anymore. That was always my fear and that's why I never got into a relationship. Semaj looked at me, "No it doesn't change anything, you are still perfect in my eyes. I'm going to take care of this?" I thought about what Kim had told me earlier, and I knew Semaj temper, "Jay, please leave it alone I don't want anything to happen to you and the future we both have ahead of us." Semaj didn't respond, and him not responding made me nervous, I didn't know if I could calm him enough for him to let this situation go. I got up, "I'm going to take a shower." I walked toward the bedroom. "Finish eating your food before it gets cold. I slaved over a hot stove all day for you, G." I joked trying to lighten the mood in the room. "You just doing your wifely duties…" Semaj started back eating the food. "Ain't no rings on these fingers." I held my left hand up as I continue to walk into the room. Semaj just looked at me laughing, "Smartass."

After Semaj ate and took a shower, he laid on the sofa to watch football. I walked out the room in a long black nightgown. "Jesus Christ, I can't stay here with you and every night you walk out here looking like you a Victoria Secret model or something." Semaj sat up on the sofa as I walked over to sit next to him. "Well, I thought you bought the stuff so I could wear it." Semaj rubbed my leg. It was something about the way he touches me, I began to get moist quickly. "Yeah you right, but damn you looking too decent." I got up to go into the kitchen and Semaj pulls me on to his lap moving his hands down to my butt. I don't know what cause me to kiss him, but I did for the first time. I had never kissed anybody before and definitely not the way I was kissing Semaj. I started feeling his manhood take a mind of its own as it begins to grow stronger and stronger. He grabbed my butt tighter squeezing it with both his hands. "Shorty, quit before we both get too deep and we can't stop." I looked at him, "Maybe I don't want to stop." Semaj picked me up and carried me to the bedroom. My heart was racing, but I knew I couldn't stop whatever was about to happen now, and I wasn't sure I even wanted to stop it at this point. Things were moving too fast and I was afraid and excited at the same time. He laid me on the bed and begin to kiss me, but he stops "Shorty, not yet you not really ready." He laid down next to me and wrap his arms around me. Which was good enough for me because I really wasn't ready for what could have just happened. The thumping between my legs was saying I was ready for all of him, but my mind wasn't there just yet. "How did you know I wasn't ready?" I looked back at Semaj. "Because I know you and I'll know when you are really ready for me to make love to you." He kissed me on the forehead "Shorty, no more secrets for real for real." I shook my head agreeing there will be no more secrets, as we laid there Semaj held me tight as he said, "Mia, I love you for real for real." I just laid there until we both fell asleep.

The next day I was happy my eyes were back to normal because the last thing I wanted to do was go to Semaj parents' house with puffy eyes. "Shorty, you about ready to slide?" Semaj walked in wearing some charcoal grey slacks and a black shirt with a black tie to match. I loved to see him dress up. I walked out the bathroom in a black knee length pencil skirt and a white button-down shirt. "Yeah, I'm ready," I was still looking in the mirror making sure everything was in place as it should be. "Shorty, what you on? You look as if something is going to walk off, you still decent. Who you trying to look decent for, you already got me?" Semaj walks up kissing me on my neck. We made it to Semaj parents mansion, and I notices the same black Bentley that picked up Sherell a couple of times before so I figured it was Uncle Steve's car. "Jay, who's all coming to dinner?" I looked at the number of cars in the driveway and began to get nervous. "Shorty, you know it's my birthday, so my O.G. invited all the family over. Don't worry Kim and Kris will be here so you won't feel uncomfortable." Semaj pinched my cheek, "I know you lowkey don't like to be around a lot of people you don't really know." "Speaking of your birthday I was going to wait to give you this, but it would actually go nicely with what you have on." I handed Semaj a wrapped boxed. He opens it, and it was a watch that we saw a couple of weeks ago while we were out. "So, you peeped me looking at this the other week. Thanks for real for real." Semaj took off the watch he had on and put this one on. He was proud of this watch. Even though he had plenty of expensive watches this one was special because it was the first time a girlfriend had ever brought him something and on top of that it was from me. He was so used to giving people he never realized that no one outside of his parents and family had ever given him anything. This was the first gift he had ever received. He knew I didn't want him for his money and this proved to him just that.

We walked in the house, and it was full of people. I

spotted one person I knew all too well, my sister Sherell. See Sherell never told me about her and Uncle Steve, even when she called to tell me Semaj came to talk to her yesterday. I made my way pass everyone to get to Sherell. I wanted to get to the bottom of this Uncle Steve and Sherell mess because Sherell was married. "Well hello sister, what are you doing here?" I asked walking over to Sherell where she was talking to a group of people. "Hi sister… let's go over here and talk." Sherell pulled me away from the crowd. "What's this mess about you and Semaj uncle dating? How is that possible, and I thought we didn't keep secrets?" I whispered looking around making sure nobody could hear me. "Mia now is not the time to talk about that." Sherell looked around as well, "No, you've been hiding this from me long enough I want to know what's going on." I wave at Mrs. Davis who was looking over at me. "Ok Mia, me and Steve have been dating and are also business partners. We both had to marry our other business partners so that we could keep them in business with us." Mia was more confused now than when she didn't know anything. "What?" Sherell laughed, "listen, Mia, Steve and I are in the drug business, and my husband and his wife are our contacts to distribute our supplies." I throw up my hand, "Ok I heard enough don't need to know anymore." Sherell looked at me, "Do you look and think of me differently" I laughed "No, I'm just happy you're not a prostitute because that's what I started to think you were." We laughed and walked back over to join Semaj and Uncle Steve talking. I enjoyed celebrating Semaj's birthday with him, his family and friends. Semaj was introducing me to everyone, and I was welcome to the family. Everything seems to be perfect for me, and for once there seem to be no more secrets between the people I loved the most and me. I felt like for once life was being kind to me, and I like that feeling.

# *FULL OF SURPRISES*

A year had passed, and things couldn't have been better. Semaj had graduated and decided that he would stay in Chicago and attend University of Illinois which was only about an hour in a half away in Champaign, Illinois. That way he was able to come home whenever he felt he needed to. This was my last year of high school and I planned to also attend University Of Illinois once I graduated. I had been going back and forth between the condo and Sherell's house, and Semaj was cool with that since he was mainly only there on the off season. My 18$^{th}$ birthday was coming up and I was excited . I didn't really have any plans, but I was just happy to be in the space I was in . "Jay, you know Mia's birthday is coming up, what you got planned for her?" Kim asked as we rode to the condo. Semaj had a bi week so he came home to spend my birthday weekend with me. "Mia get shit year round I'm not thinking about shorty, and whatever it is I'm not telling you so you can tell her." Semaj said joking. "Naw, but I'm going to tell you because I'm going to need your help." "Jay, don't go all out because I don't like all that attention and you know that." I told him as we pulled up. The condo had become our little hang out spot. Kim would have Rickey meet her there and whoever Kris was into at the moment would sometimes come over. Rickey was on the football team with Semaj and Kris so they were all cool with each other. "Jay, I think that's Brittney running off over there." Kris points to a girl running around the building. "I told Jay I thought I saw her across the street last week, but he thought I was tripping." I told them as we got ready to walk in. "Mr. Davis, a young lady was just hear requesting information about you and your residents here." The doorman told Semaj as we walk to the elevators. We all looked over at Semaj, "Man what? I ain't never bring her here." Semaj said as he looked at me. "Kris, you know how that chick is, every time I try to leave her along and start messing with somebody else." Kris shook his head, "Yeah she a real goofy for real for real." We walk into the house and didn't think anything else about it.

I cooked and everybody was eating and laughing as Semaj cell phone rings. "Mia answer that." Semaj yell because the phone was in the bedroom where me and Kim was while the guys where in the living room playing the game. I looked at the phone and it was an unsaved number calling, "Hello," I answered it. "Where Semaj at and why you answering his phone?" Brittney barked on the other side of the phone. Laughing I ask, "When you going to give it up. We saw you running from OUR house today." "Girl, you and Semaj, don't live together I don't know what you talking about, besides I was just with him last night so you don't matter. I know you can never give him what I give." Brittney yell through the phone. While walking into the living room to let Semaj deal with his problem, "You're absolutely right I could never give him some run down pussy that everybody with a dollar has had. And if you're ok with him coming by there getting his rocks off and then coming back to me giving me the world that's good for you." I said before throwing the phone at Semaj's head. "Mia what the hell?" Semaj yell as he caught the phone right before it hit him. "Handle that before it becomes a problem." I told Semaj as I walked back into the room.

Semaj knew that when I was upset I could be ruthless because he seen it a couple of times, so when the phone came flying at his head he had a feeling he knew exactly who it was. "G, Mia gone beat your ass you better handle this problem real quick." Kris joke with Semaj. "Man, Shorty know not to play with me," Semaj said as he finally put the phone to his ear, "Yo, who this?" "So, you really taking this chick serious I see…Letting her answer your phone and everything." Brittney said to him. "Man, I knew it was you, dam" Semaj said as he hung up in her face. "Jay, you not still poking Brittney are you?" Kris asked as I walked back out the room to the living room. "Hell no, I been stop messing with her, it's been almost two years. I'm not trying to do anything to hurt Mia for real for real." Semaj said noticing me walking into the kitchen. "A Shorty, what she said to you that got you so pressed man?" He walked into the kitchen blocking me from getting into the refrigerator. "Jay, move out the way, it don't matter what she said, I'm good." I said and they all laugh as Rickey said, "Mia if that's how you hand someone the phone when you good, please make sure I'm nowhere around when you are pressed for real for real." They all laughed Kris joined in on the joke, "Mia you sure your daddy ain't no professional baseball player. The way you threw that phone at Jay head pitching has to be in your bloodline." We all laugh, "We'll talk later," Semaj whispered in my ear then kissing me on my cheek before going back over to entertain his guest.

Later that night while everybody was in the living room watching tv I went to take a nice bubble bath. Not too long after I had got in the tub Semaj came in the bathroom. "So, you ready to tell me what that was all about earlier?" He asked as he held his hand out for me to give him my rag so he could wash my back. "I'm just trying to figure out how she knew that we still haven't had sex or anything yet? And if you not messing with her no more why would she say yall was together last night?" I said as he started rubbing my back. "Mia, think about what you saying, where was I at last night?" Semaj had a point he was with me and I couldn't believe I allowed this crazy chick to get to me. "Shorty stop letting that goofy press you, I ain't never lied to you before so why would I start now. Don't let this goofy get to you, I don't mess with that girl and you know that. You see she had to call from a different number cause I wasn't answering the phone for her period." Semaj said as he started to bathe me all over, "Jay what you doing." I tried to grab his hand to stop him, but he snatched away from me, "Stop playing with me Mia, just relax man." He said as he began to rub the rag over my breast. Thank goodness I was already sitting in water because I instantly became wet I closed my eyes and let out a soft moan. He moved down to my stomach and right as he got between my legs he stop, "You got the rest shorty." He said as he smile and walked to the bathroom. "Get out!" I scream throwing water at him. "What happen, Mia?" He laughed and walked out the door leaving me sitting in the tub hot and bothered once again. This dam boy knows exactly what he's doing I thought as I finish bathing myself, and got out the tub.

After I got out the tub, I went in the guest room where Kim was laying down watching tv. "Kim…" I sat down on the bed. "What's wrong Mia?" Kim asked, she knew me too well. "Wait I want to tell all yall at one time." I picked up the phone and call Chari who then called Ronyette, and on the cell phone I called my sisters India and Toya. "Okay Mia you got all our attention now, what's the problem?" Kim asked. "I know what the problem is she let Semaj hit," Chari said as everybody laughed. "No I didn't let him hit, but I think I'm finally ready." "What?" They all said together as if it was planned. "Wait a minute what happen to waiting until after you finish high school." My sister India said. "Listen you must not have seen Semaj, that boy is fine. Mia don't get mad I'm just telling the truth. I know you get territorial about what's yours and stuff." Ronyette said as we all laugh. "No, but for real yall, I think I'm ready, what should I do?" I asked. "Nothing, just let it happen when it happens," my sister Toya said, "Trust me it's only a matter of time before it happens. Semaj isn't going to be able to keep controlling himself around you. Mia have you looked at yourself naked in the mirror lately?" Kim added, "Besides I heard him and Kris talking the other night while you was sleep and your sister is right, he's about to lose it sooner or later." "Shorty, I'll be back I'm about to take Rickey home, you riding or you staying here." Semaj interrupted us. "Hi Semaj" they all said in a teasing way. He laugh, "What's good," he said walking off. "I'm coming give me a minute." I told him. "Well I will talk to you all later." I said hanging up the phone. "Kim how long was Jay standing there, and you better not lie?" I asked as we walked out the room. "I'm not sure, but I think he heard us. When I looked up he was there and told me to be quiet." Kim said as we walked out the door to meet them downstairs. Shaking my head, I looked at him, "You so nosey you just can't help it." I said to him as I got in the car. Laughing he looked at me and said, "I don't know what you talking about. You ready?" I looked at him, "You ready… to go?" We both laughed. I knew he had heard everything from that comment, and I was happy he knew.

After dropping Rickey off we went back to the condo and got ready for bed. "So you think you ready, Shorty?" Semaj hugged me from behind as I fixed my hair. "Why you always being nosey man," I asked him leaning back on him looking up to him. "Answer my question, Mia" he looked back down at me. "That's what you heard me say right." He laughed, "Mia your ass always avoid answering a question." I smiled, "Hopefully we both will find out sooner than later if I'm ready or not." I said as I grab his dick and walked off. I had never attempted to touch him there before tonight. "Oh yeah, she ready." Semaj said following behind me. We ended our night and conversation at that.

It was Saturday and it was my birthday. I always got excited about my birthday. My dad was always the first person to call me every year on the day of my birthday "Happy birthday baby girl." My dad said as I answered the phone. "Thank you daddy, what are you doing." I asked as I got dress. Semaj was taking me out to breakfast. "Nothing much, what does Semaj have planned for you." My dad asked. He had come up and met Semaj over the summer. "Daddy I don't know Semaj always has something up his sleeves." I told him as Semaj walked back in the house. "Well I like Semaj, he's a good kid." I smile looking over at Semaj as he sat down not knowing I was even looking at him. "Yeah, he's alright. Daddy I have to go I'll call you later. Love you." I hung up the phone and continue getting dress. Before heading out the door that morning I had spoke with all most everyone that was important to me.

After breakfast I went and got pampered getting my hair done, and a manicure and pedicure. Semaj was on the phone more than normal today, so I knew he was up to something. I walked out the hair salon and Semaj was on the phone again. "Yeah be there at 8:30," he saw me walking up and rushed off the phone. "Why every time I come around you rush off the phone?" I said getting in the car. "You look beautiful as always." Semaj said closing the door. He was changing the subject, "Jay so you pulling a me on me. Man, what you got plan?" I said has he got in the car. "Mia, why you always have to know everything and be in control all the time," he said as we pulled off.

When we got back to the condo there were a couple of gifts laid out on the bed. I looked back at Semaj and he smiled, "What it's not my birthday they not for me." I walked over to the bed and open the first gift it was an off the shoulder purple floor length dress. I looked at Semaj again and he pointed to the next package for me to open. That box had a pair of sliver pumps in it, and the last box was smaller then the other two. I opened it and it held the most beautiful pair of 2ct diamond earrings I had ever seen with a chain and pedant to match. "Jay, they are beautiful, but you didn't have to do this." I hug him as I gave him a kiss. "This is just the start it's your day shorty, you get whatever you want today. Now go get dress we're having dinner at pops and my O.G. house tonight." We both started getting dress and I could only imagine what Semaj and Kim had planned those two together it was no telling what was going to happen tonight.

We pulled up to Mr. and Mrs. Davis mansion, and just like I thought it was something going on. "Semaj, who's all here I thought you said just us, ma and pops?" I had started building a great relationship with Semaj's parents. "Yeah, it is..." Semaj smiled. "No....I know that smile and I see Uncle Steve's car and there's Kris car too." I said as I looked around at the cars parked in front of the house. "Man shorty, stop trying to figure shit out and just trust me." Semaj said as he helped me out of the car. "Well stop trying to surprise me all the dam time and tell me what's going on," I said as he closed the door. "Mia, don't start this shit," Semaj said and I decided I'll let him have this one instead of ruining whatever he had planned, "Ok, I'm going to go with the flow," I said walking up to the door.

Semaj opened the door and it was dark in the house. We walked into the kitchen and it was still dark. "Why is it so dark and where is everybody at?" I grab Semaj arm as he led me to the back yard by the pool where I started to see lights finally. "SURPRISE!!!!!" Everybody screams and caught me by surprise. I was shocked as I looked around, I scream, "DADDY!!! TAMARA!!!" walking over to them still looking around I noticed my two sisters, India and Toya. I walked as fast as I could because the dress was skin tight so I couldn't run. I got to them and gave them a hug and when I turned around there was Chari and Ronyette standing behind me. "I just talk to you all last night, and yall didn't even tell me about this." I said as they laugh, "Mia, you don't have to always be in control," my sister Toya said. I looked at Semaj would was standing talking to Pops and I could tell he had more surprises. Pops what time it's going to be here?" I heard Semaj saying as I walked back toward him. "What else you got planned, Jay. You've done enough." I told him as I gave him a kiss. Mr. Davis said, "Mia, I think you miss someone," as he pointed over to the outdoor kitchen. I turned and looked, and there was my mom. We met each other halfway and embraced each other. Semaj had everybody there that I loved. "Momma, Semaj got you here, too." "No, it was Sherell who got me here." My mom said pointing to Sherell who was standing there smiling. I smiled back and mouthed "Thank you."

We all had a good time, but it was something that had Semaj attention most of the night and I didn't know what it was. "Jay, what you got going on you been focus on something else all night?" looking around I didn't see Kim, "And where did Kim go," I asked as I went a sat by Semaj who was just getting off the phone for the hundred time that night. "Mia, just trust me the night is not over yet." Semaj stands up and gets everyone's attention. "Excuse me everyone, I want to thank everyone for coming. Mr. Andre, thank you for trusting me to take care of Mia and I plan to continue doing so for the rest of my life. Mrs. Lisa, thank you for giving birth to the most beautiful person I have ever seen." Everybody there was aweing at the words he was saying as he continue, "Mia, I told you when you finally gave me the chance to talk to you," he looked back toward everybody, "she made me chase her for almost four years," everybody laughed. He turned back to me, "I told you that you were my future wife and I meant that, and still do." Everybody got excited. "No, I'm not about to ask Mia to marry me just yet, but I do have a surprise for her. If everybody would follow me to the front of the house."

Semaj held my hand as we walked to the front of the house. Semaj and I were the last ones to walk out the door, and in front of the house there was a brand new black BMW. I screamed, "Jay who car is that?" I asked as Pops walked over to me handing me the keys. "Happy birthday Mia, this is from all five of your parents and Jay." I looked over at my dad, my mom, my bonus mom, and Mrs. Davis and they were just smiling. Pops continue, "Mia, you deserve this and so much more is to come for you." I began to cry, Kim and Chari ran over to me, "No you not about to cry," they said as they wiped my eyes. I looked over at Semaj and smiled, "I'm going to get you. Why...." before I could even ask the question he walked me over to the car and said, "Why not you Mia?" Grabbing my hand and turning to the crowd he continue, "Thank you all for coming enjoy the rest of the night, but I have another surprise for the birthday girl so we about to spin." Opening the car door on my new car I got in the passenger side as Semaj walked around to drive, "She'll see yall tomorrow." He jumped in the car and off we went. "Jay, you really out did yourself for real." I said as we pulled off. "It's not over yet." Semaj said kissing my hand. I didn't ask any more questions because I knew if I asked he wasn't going to tell me anyway. So I just went with the flow and enjoy the ride.

We pulled back up to the condo, and got out the car. He opened the door and I saw rose petals all over the floor with candles everywhere. "Jay, what you got planned." I asked as I walked in looking around. He didn't say anything he just took my hand and walked me into the house. We walked over to the living room and Jagged Edge started playing as Semaj swung me around into him. I shook my head and laughed because it seem he was always pulling something out the hat to amaze me. We began to dance as he began to sing.

**"Is it real... what I feel could it be you and me till the end of time? Take my heart hold it tight; it's true love. You know I gotta be...."** I started to sing with him, **"I gotta be the one you touch. Baby I gotta be the one you love....."**

I laid my head on Semaj's chest and I said a quiet prayer, "God thank you for allowing me to see 18 years of life and although all 18 have not been good to me, I thank you for letting me find someone who treats me like a queen and for letting me know that my life was not a mistake. Thank you for letting me be able to finally trust and love someone. Thank you for letting me fall in love with this man, my man. Amen." We dance and just enjoy Jagged Edge as they continue to sing their hit "I gotta Be". Semaj stopped dancing and looked down at me, "Mia I love you shorty for real for real." I looked back up at Semaj, "I love you too," I said for the first time. I was finally able to admit that I was in love.

"Now, you ready." he grab my hand and walked me to the bedroom. "Ready for what ?" I asked confused as we walked into the room and suddenly stop. I had never saw a room set up so romantic. There were candles that led to the bathroom and to the bed and rose petals were everywhere. "Who did this Jay, what do you have plan now." He put his finger up to my lips. "You trust me, Shorty." He asked as he faced me pulling me toward the bathroom smiling. I just laughed and went with whatever he had planned. We walked into the bathroom and there was lit candles all around the tub. I looked over at Semaj who was checking the water to make sure it was still hot. He looked up at me and smiled, "Come here," he said.

# SURE YOU READY

I walked over to him  as he stood up behind me. He unzipped my dress as he normally would when we came from going out. I stepped out of it letting it fall to the floor. He unclipped my bra as he said, "Take those off," pointing down to my panties. I slid them down as I stepped into the tub. Semaj stood there for a minute as if he was trying to make sure this was the right time. "You getting in," I asked as I sat down. "Mia, are you sure you ready?" He asked as he started to take off his clothes. "We will find out tonight won't we?" I said as I watch Semaj get undress. This was a fine man. I hadn't seen a men fully naked in person, but this one here was a special type of man. He was fully and truly blessed in more ways than one. As he got in the tub I thought to myself, thank god I shaved earlier. When Sherell found out me and Semaj was dating she told me to always keep my little lady clean, trim, and neat. She said you never know when you made have to show it to someone.

Semaj got in the tub behind me for the first time. He began to wash my back. I said to him looking him in his eyes, "I'm scared." He kissed me and said, "I got you, I promise I won't hurt you." I turned back around and exhaled as he continue to bathe me. When he got to my inner thighs he slowly rub his fingers down the middle of my clit that cause my hormones to take a mind of their own. After he finish bathing me he turned me around to sit on his lap, he kissed me again before asking, "Mia are you sure." I wrapped my arms around his neck and kissed him before sitting down as he slid inside of me. "Shit" he moan as he grip my butt and our bodies moved in rhythm with the water. I moan, something that was once so painful to me had become so much pleasure in that moment. I suddenly stop, "Semaj, get a condom." He stood up while holding me stepping out of the tub and walking over to the bed. "You good I got you," Semaj said as he laid me on the bed and began kissing me from my neck working his way down to my breast. I moaned and jumped a little. He looked up at me, "Mia, I told you I was going to make you love me." He worked his way back up kissing me with so much passion as he slid back inside of me gently. I moan, "I love you, Jay." That night I learn new things about the body that I had never known as we made love all night to our own music.

Morning came and I looked over at a naked Semaj remembering what had to place, I smiled not realizing that he was woke, "Mia, you know you lost your virginity last night." I looked at him like he was crazy, "Jay, stop playing you know what happen to me." I said as I walked into the bathroom. "That shit don't matter, you always been a virgin in my eyes and I was your first." Semaj yelled from the bed.

I laughed he was right, he was my first everything and I couldn't be more happier. I turned the shower on and got in. While I was in the shower Semaj came in the bathroom. "Shorty, so now you ready to have my baby?" I didn't know where the question came from out the blue. I know we had talked about it a couple of times, but that was it. "Semaj, stop playing. Yeah I'll have your baby later on down the road." He laughed, "Later may be sooner than you think," he walks out the bathroom as I finish taking my shower. Then it hit me, this fool didn't put on the condom when I told him to. "Semaj, come here," I screamed as I walked into the bedroom looking in the nightstand where we kept two condoms just in case we ever got to this point, and they both were still in the draw. Semaj walked into the room and saw me looking in the draw and started laughing, "What's up Shorty, I'm trying to clean all these rose petals up," Semaj walked over to the draw and closed it. "Jay, why didn't you put on the condom last night." He pushes me on to the bed standing over me as he put his hand between my legs, "Because I wanted to feel all of you," kissing me as he played inside of me with his finger. I became wet, "Jay, we have to go we don't have time." He took his fingers out as he kissed me sliding inside of me, "I always have time to make sure you're happy and satisfied." I felt every stroke and motion he made and it felt so good. Realizing he was about to nut, I try to stop him, because again he didn't put on a condom. He lean over as he came and whispered, "You got pregnant last night, so this nut doesn't matter." He kissed me and laid next to me. I looked over at him , "Jay, what if I get pregnant for real ." He looked over and smile at me, "Well I guess you'll be my babymomma." I hated that term and he knew that , "I'm not no damn babymomma, stop playing with me," I headed to get back in the shower. "Mia, you know you will never just be a babymomma. Stop tripping, you good no matter what happen. If you get pregnant or not I'm not going nowhere." Semaj said as he got up to get in the shower with me.

After we clean the house and got everything back to normal we headed over to Semaj's parents' house. On the ride over we talked about what had took place last night. "Thank you for making me wait until you was ready, Mia." Semaj said as he looked over at me. "I told you I was worth the wait," I liked to talk trash about how good I was in bed, but honestly I didn't know if it was good or not. "But for real shorty, you must have a pot of gold between your legs cause I ain't never had a kitty boost like that." Semaj said as I laughed kind of embarrassed and proud at the same time. "Jay, thank you for everything you have ever done for me. Last night was everything I ever wanted my first time to be like." I said as we pulled up to the house. "I was not about to let nobody else end up with you. From the first day I saw you I knew you was something special and was send here just for me," he told me as we walked up to the front door.

Inside the house everything was set up so nice for brunch. "Yall late, what yall did last night," Kim said as she walked over to us smiling. I look back at Semaj and laughed, "I take it she's the one who set up everything last night while we were here." Turning back to Kim, "Thank you, Kim I love you." Kim hugged me "Girl I don't know what you talking about, what happen?" Kim tease, knowing she knew exactly what I was talking about. Semaj walked over to where Kris and his dad was standing, while me and Kim headed to where the food was at. Everyone had went back to Miami except India and Toya.

"So son, did you make me a grandbaby last night." Mr. Davis joked as Semaj joined him and Kris. "I sure hope so pops." Semaj said giving his dad five. "So was it worth the wait," Kris asked. "Hell yeah," Semaj said as they laugh, "I'll wait another 3 years if I have to do it all over again with Mia. I never had a kitty boost like that since I started poking." They went to sit down, "Jay, I told you when you find true love everything about her would be different from what you're used to," Mr. Davis told Semaj. "Man pops, I thought I was in love with Mia before, now I know I am for real. I have never took the risk of getting any chick pregnant. I always strapped up, and for me to not attempt to look over at the condoms that we both agreed to keep in the house for if this was to ever happen." Semaj said shaking his head. "Wait does Mia know you didn't use it," Kris asked. "She knew afterwards when she looked in the draw and saw them still sitting there." They laughed. "If I know Mia she was pissed," Mr. Davis said. "Pops she wasn't as mad as I thought she was going to be. Mia know I'm not going nowhere." Semaj said as I walked over. "Pops, what yall talking about?" I asked looking at them giving them the side-eye. "Hey baby girl, we just talking about the grandbaby." Mr. Davis laughed, "Pops, that's not funny. Jay, you can't hold water." I said slapping him in the head walking away. "I love you shorty." Semaj yelled behind me. "Whatever," I said as I kept walking back over to where Kim and my sisters where sitting. I knew his dad and Kris would be the first to know, those where his two best friends.

"So, are you going to tell us what happen or do we have to go hear it from Semaj too," Kim said as I sat down. "Well we can tell from that smile and glow all over her face it must have been good," India said. "It was more then I could have ever imagine." I said reminiscing about last night. "Well dang, what did Semaj do?" Toya asked sitting up. "Let's just leave all that to the imagination," I told them as I got up to walk off. I didn't like going into details about personal things, and I felt like some things should be kept private. "We going to get the details from Semaj, you always holding back." Kim said as we all walked into the house.

While we were all hanging out after eating there was a knock on the door. "I got it," Semaj said as he walked to the door and everyone else continue to play cards. He opens the door, "Hi I missed you," Brittney grabs on to Semaj as he tries to push her off of him and out the door before anyone knows it's her. "You tweaking what you doing here?" Semaj said looking behind him making sure no one saw her as he closed the door. "Semaj, I know you miss poking me. Can't nobody give you a kitty boost like me. Besides I know you still not poking lame as Mia yet," Brittney said as she tried to kiss him. "G, you need to spin for real for real. You already know I'm not on that with you no more. Plus, if Mia come out here you gone have a bigger problem than you can handle, she gone end up beating your ass for real for real" Semaj said as he push Brittney again. "How you even get pass the security to get in here," Semaj asked as I walked out the door. "Girl, you just don't give up, do you?" I laughed scaring both of them. Semaj, walked over to grab me, "Mia I got this." I snatched away, "Apparently not, because the chick wouldn't be standing here right now if you handle this before like I told you too." I was the one usually doing all the calming down, but today it was me who had to be calmed down. "Mia, I got this, you coolin." Semaj said kissing me in front of Brittney. "Really Semaj you just gone try me like that again for this bitch." "Spin goofy for real for real, I don't know what's wrong with you," Semaj said as we walked back in the house.

After that I was ready to go home and just lay down. We

drop Toya and India off to the airport before heading back to the condo. While pulling up to the condo I turned and asked, "Semaj, are you sure you not messing with that girl no more." Semaj looked at me as if I was crazy, "What?!!" He jumped out the car as we stopped, "Mia, get out the car." He pulled me over to the side of the building that led to the beach. He stop as we got to the water where there was a beach chair. He pushed me onto the beach chair as he climbed on top of me. "Do this look and feel like I want someone else, but you," Semaj pulled my skirt up, ripping my panties off and began making love to me right there on the beach. "Semaj, people are going to see us." I try to stop him. "So what, let them watch." I laid back and join the show. After making me cum a couple of times, we went upstairs and made more love until we fell asleep.

# MADE THROUGH LOVE

It had been almost two months since Semaj and I started having sex. He was coming home more often ever since. Football season was over and he was out for the Christmas break, and we both was loving it. I walked in the condo coming back from the store, out of breath and barely able to fit in my jeans. "Damn, Mia your hips are spreading," Kim said as she walked over to help with the bags. "Shut up Kim, I don't know what's going on with my body," I said as I looked around. "Girl , they say your hips start spreading when you start making love," we laugh, "Where's Jay?" I asked as I unbutton my jeans and sat down. "She pregnant that's all her problem is," Semaj came from out of the bedroom walking over rubbing my stomach. I slap his hand away, "Stop telling people that before someone believes you." "I don't know Mia, you have put on a couple of pounds and you was sick every morning last week," Kim said looking at my stomach and then at Semaj. "Really Kim," I walked off. "Shorty, you didn't tell me you was sick last week," Semaj said following me into the room. "Because it wasn't that serious to tell you about," I took off my jeans and put on a pair of sweatpants. I caught Semaj looking at me smiling, "Jay, I'm not pregnant stop it." "We will see, babymomma," Semaj said rubbing my stomach and walking off. I walked out behind him, "What is that smell, what are you cooking?" I asked Kim who was cooking. "Mia that's just fried chicken," they all laughed, "Semaj you might be right," Kris joked. "I'm not about to be the butt of yall jokes, I'm going to lay down." I said turning around going back into the bedroom. Laying in the bed I thought to myself, what if I am pregnant? What am I going to do about going to college and raising a baby. I fell off to sleep for about an hour before Semaj came and woke me up, "Shorty, come eat." I got up and walked into the bathroom. "Jay I'm not feeling good." I brushed my teeth then walked back into the living room. The smell of the food hit me and I ran to the bathroom as Semaj followed me. I made it to the toilet just in time before throwing up all that I had ate that day. I looked up as Semaj handed me a warm towel, "It's a stomach virus." Semaj laughed, "Alright, Mia whatever you want to tell yourself," he said as he walked off. After getting myself together I went and laid on the sofa as Semaj and Kris was playing the game. "Shorty, how you feeling," Semaj leaned over kissing me. "I'm ok just tired," I said as I sat up so he could sit down and I laid on his lap. He rub my stomach. "Jay, I'm not pregnant I just have a stomach virus," I tried to convince myself more than Semaj.

For the next couple of days I was feeling a little better, but still wasn't feeling back to myself. I couldn't shake this virus for nothing. I never took medicine so that was out the question, so all I could do is lay and bed and wait for it to pass through my body. I was happy school was out for break because the mornings was the worst. Semaj came back in from the store, as I was finally getting out the bed. "Shorty, I got something for you to take." Semaj turned around handing me a pregnancy test. I bust out laughing, "Jay, I'm not taking this," still laughing as I took the test and looked at it. "Mia, what's so bad about you having my baby," he asked. "Nothing, if I was pregnant, but I'm not," I said as I walked to the bathroom and put the test under the counter. If I was going to take the test it will be when I am ready to.

We were getting ready to go and have dinner over to Semaj's parents house. We made it over to Semaj's parents house and as soon as the door open the smell of the food hit me and I was instantly sick to my stomach. I kicked off my shoes and ran down the hall to the bathroom. "Jay, what's wrong with Mia," Mrs. Davis asked, "Hey ma, Mia hasn't been feeling good." Semaj didn't want to tell his parents just yet that he thinks Mia is pregnant even though he knew she was. They walked into the kitchen and I finally was about to get myself together to join them. "Hi ma and pops, I am sorry. I been sick for the past couple of days with some type of stomach virus." I said as I give them a hug. "Mia, you sure it's just a stomach virus," Mrs. Davis said rubbing my stomach and pinching my hips. I laughed, "Ma, not you too." I said as I sat down at the table. "Ma, I got her a test, but she won't take it," Semaj started eating, "I don't know why yall want me to have a baby so bad." I laughed as I drunk a glass of water. "Because we need someone else to spoil. We tired of just spoiling you two,"

Mr. Davis joked and we all laughed.

As we're driving home I asked, "Jay, you really think I'm pregnant?" Semaj looked at me and smiled, "Mia I told you, you was pregnant the day after it happened. You just didn't believe me." I rolled my eyes, "So, you an OBGYN now," we laughed. We pulled up to the condo, there was a familiar face standing in front of the building. "What you on, my G?" Semaj jumped out the car before he fully stopped it. "Oh, so this where you got this bitch living at now. Wow, all I used to get was a cheap hotel room if that?" Brittney stood in front of the building entrance. "Maybe, you should've up the value of your pussy, and things may have been different," I said as I walked passed Brittney and into the building not even looking in her direction. "How you know where we stay at, what you a stalker, now?" Semaj asked as he held the door for me to walk in. "So, you just treat her like she some goddess or Queen." Brittney looked at me with pure jealousy and hatred in her eyes. She wants what I was getting, and she was planning to get it by any means necessary. "She is my Queen and you need to spin and never come thru here again, or it's gone pop off, OMS for real for real," Semaj said. "You can't protect her forever" Brittney looked through the doors at me as I wait for the elevator. "Goofy, you tweaking for real for real. I'll protect her by any means necessary." Semaj walked in to join me. "Careful wouldn't want the breaks to go out on that pretty black BMW you just bought your girl for her birthday." Brittney yells as the doors closed. Semaj was heading back to the door, but I grab his arm pulling him onto the elevator, "You sure know how to pick them." We laughed and went inside. "Why does she just keep popping up out of nowhere?" I went into the kitchen looking for something to eat. "Shorty, I have no idea," Semaj sat on the sofa, "It seems like the deeper we get in a relationship, the more she becomes obsessed with you and what we got," Semaj walked over to get something the drink. "I'm not worried about that girl, she's your problem, not mine. You better get rid of her. I don't know what you did to her when you poked her, but the way she's acting," I laughed thinking about how crazy Brittney had been acting. The phone rang and caught them both by surprise. "Yo!" Semaj always answered the phone like that and I couldn't stand it. "Make sure you let your girl know I can have you whenever I want you." It was Brittney. "Man, you a goofy for real for real. How you get our number? Don't call our house no more!" Semaj slammed the phone down. "Shorty make sure you change the number, this mug tripping for real for real." Semaj went to look out the window. "Jay, who was that?" I stood in the kitchen eating my ice cream. "Shorty, that crazy chick," Semaj said. "And you want me to have a baby, and this chick is still running around here acting like she still messing with you." I said looking up and jumping, "Semaj stop walking up on me like that," he stood in front of me, "Mia what you trying to say, you gone get rid of my baby," I looked at him as if he was crazy, "That thought never even came to my mind. Besides I'm not pregnant."

Christmas was in a day and I still wasn't feeling any better. Semaj laid in bed sleep while I walked to the bathroom. I looked on the counter and saw the test. I guess Semaj had put it there. What the hell I might as well take it. I followed the direction that were on the box. I placed the stick on the countertop and it didn't take more then a minute for two lines to show up. "Oh my god," I said in disbelief, I was pregnant. I decided not to tell Semaj just yet. I took the test and put it in my closet so that Semaj wouldn't find it until I could decide how to tell him. I went and got back in the bed and went back to sleep.

That morning while Semaj was still sleep I figured out how I would tell Semaj. "Jay, wake up," I walked over to him holding a wrap box. "Shorty, that gift could've waited til later." Semaj grab the box still half sleep. I sat down on the bed as he opened it. "I think you really want this one." Jumping up as he pulled out what was in the box he scream, "I knew it...I told you," he kissed me with so much passion, "Come let me feed my babies," he laid me down as I looked at him like he lost his mind, "you mean baby without an s on the end right." He smiled that smiled that probably was the reason I ended up pregnant, "Mia you gone learn to listen to me." He kissed me and we celebrated the life that we had created together.

Later that day we got ready to head over to the Davis annual Christmas sweater party they had every Christmas. "Jay, do not go in here telling everybody I'm pregnant. Let's wait until after the holidays please, Jay." I said to Semaj before I got out the car. "Shorty, I can't keep nothing like that from Ma and Pops you know that." I looked around and notice we were the first ones there. "Ok lets go tell them before everybody gets here." As we walk to the door Semaj said, "Good because I didn't want to have brought this for nothing," pulling the home test out his pocket. I couldn't help but laugh, "Really Jay, you brought the test with you." I shook my head as we walk inside, "I can't believe you." We walked into the family room where ma and pops where sitting, "There goes my two favorite people." Mrs. Davis said as we walked over to sit with them. "Hi ma...hi pops," I sat down next to Semaj. "Jay why you look like you got something to say," Pops asked as he look back and forth between Semaj and I. "Sabrina they got something to tell us," Pops said as he turned the tv off. "No Semaj has something to tell yall, not me," I said directing all the attention to Semaj. "Well we came early to talk to yall before everybody got here." Semaj stood up pulling the box that held the test in it out his pocket. He handed it to his mom, "This was my Christmas gift that Mia gave me this morning," Mrs. Davis opened it and screamed, "Miaaaaa…..I knew it," she jumped up handing the test to Mr. Davis as she said, "James we're having a baby." I couldn't help but laugh. "I never seen parents so happy that their child was having a baby." "No, we're just happy we get to keep you in the family forever now." Pops said joking, "You see before you Semaj just picked anything to mess around with." We all laughed. "No but ma and pops we are only telling yall for right now until after we go to the doctor and see how everything is going." Semaj told them right before the doorbell ring. "Your secret is safe with me." Mrs. Davis said as she went to open the door as the guest start to arrive.

I had become very sensitive to smell so I tried to stay away from the food and people with strong perfume. Kim noticing that I wasn't really moving from where I was sitting. Her and Sherell walked over to me at the same time. "Mia are you ok you haven't moved from this spot all night," Sherell said as she sat down. "What kind of perfume do you have on," I tried to play it off by saying, "It smells good." But Sherell knew I was lying because it showed all over my face. "Mia, have you still been sick?" Kim asked me. "Look what Semaj got me for Christmas," I said showing them a bracelet I had got. "That's nice, but you haven't answered the question Mia," Sherell said. "Yall stop trying to make me have a baby so soon," I laughed as I walked off. "I don't know who she think she fooling," Kim said as her and Sherell followed me over to where Semaj and the rest of the family was.

I stood leaning my head on Semaj's shoulder, "How you feeling?" Semaj asked me. "I need to lay down I can't take all these different types of smells," I told him in his ear. I didn't want to leave the party because it would be too obvious, so I decided to go upstairs to Semaj's room and lay down. While I was laying down Mrs. Davis came up to check on me, "Mia how are you feeling?" she sat down on the edge of the bed. I sat up and smile, "I'm ok, I guess." Besides being sick every day for the last three weeks I was fine. "No, I mean how do you feel about being pregnant?" She looked at me as she asked me. "I really haven't giving it much thought. I took the test at four this morning. I told Jay, and then we got ready to come here." I said looking at her, "I'm scared, but happy I guess." She came closer and rubbed my head, "Mia, you don't have to be scared we will always be here for you. I know you went through a lot growing up so it's ok for you to feel afraid, but my son worships the ground you walk on." She sat back down and smile, "It's funny because I was in your shoes at only 15 years old and it was James's mom sitting here where I am now." Just as she said that Semaj grandmother came in the room, "Mia, how far along are you?" Mrs. Davis and I both looked over at her, "Grandma Pearl, what are you talking about," She walked over and sat down next to Mrs. Davis, "Girl I know a pregnant woman when I see one. I had four sons, all before I was twenty-four, and two of them had babies in high school," pointing over at Mrs. Davis, "the same talk she giving you, who you think taught her the speech." We all laugh. Grandma Pearl added as the door was opening, "You're life isn't over. You have a whole family behind you. I'm only 60 I got a lot more years in me to be here for yall." We laugh again as I started to get up out the bed Semaj enter the room, "The three loves of my life in one room," Semaj bends over kissing his grandma, "Boy, you done knock this girl up, now what's your plan," Semaj looks at me, "I thought we wasn't telling nobody yet." Grandma Pearl cut in, "she ain't tell me boy, I know when somebody pregnant or not," she looked back at me, "I knew she was pregnant when she wouldn't move out that one spot all night and every time somebody would come by her she had to keep herself from throwing up." Semaj came and sat on the other side of me. He looked down at my stomach as he rubbed it, "Grandma you know I'm going to take care of my babies and Mia," I cut him off, "Will you stop saying babies, it's only one baby in there," They all laugh, "What's funny," I asked trying to see what I missed. Grandma Pearl stop laughing, "Jay maybe right, I'm a twin, James and Steve are twins. Semaj was a twin, but his twin passed away due to complications. So, it's possible you could be having two." They all started back laughing, but I wasn't. "Yall just can't be satisfied. You wanted me to be pregnant, now I'm pregnant that's not good enough, now yall want me to have twins. I can't make yall happy I see," I said joking as they all laughed.

The next couple weeks my sickness had began to get better and I was able to enjoy the remaining time of Semaj being home before he had to go back to campus. I finally told Sherell and Kim what it seem everybody already knew, so they had been coming over to the condo that I was now staying at full time. "So how does it feel to know that you are going to be a mommy soon," Kim asked me as I laid on the sofa. "I don't know yet nothing has change as of yet. I'm just scared that things will change between Semaj and I." Semaj and Kris walked in, "Babymomma, how you feeling," Kris said playing around. "I'm good for now, what you got to eat, Jay," I asked as I got up motioning for Semaj to meet me in the bedroom. "What's up, Shorty ," he asked. "Jay, we got a problem." I said as I sat on the bed. "What happen, you good," he sat next to me rubbing on me, which automatically did something to me, "Stop Jay, for real your girl was standing outside when I pulled up earlier again today." I told him grabbing his hand. "Man you serious," he said as he grab the phone. "Jay, who you calling," I asked as the phone started ringing. "Hello, I knew you would call. What your queen still ain't busting it open yet, so you want this old thing back," it was Brittney. "Yo, stop all that bullshit, I'm good with mine and what I got. I just called to tell you stop coming around here, I'm dead ass," Semaj told her and hung up the phone. "That ain't gone stop her watch," I said as I walked to the bathroom.

I started back feeling like myself right after New Year. I was so thankful, because Semaj was headed back to school, so he had Kim to come and stay with me in the condo while he was away he didn't feel I needed to be by myself. I still looked normal so no one knew I was pregnant when I went back to school and I wanted to keep it that way. We called my parents and told them the day after Christmas, so all the important people knew and that's how I liked it. I made an appointment for the doctor the following month that way Semaj would be able to go with me. He wanted to make sure he was part of everything dealing with this pregnancy. I guess most people would say I was bless with a good life after all.

# OTHER PLANS

I am five months pregnant and we are on our way to find out what we are having. So far everything has been great for me. The doctor has hinted that she has heard two heartbeats a couple of times, but today will be the day we find out. "Let's make a deal. If it's twins we have to get married right after you graduate school and if it's one baby I'll buy you a that new Porsche Cayenne you been looking at," Semaj told me as we waited for the doctor to call us to the back. "Ok, deal cause it's only one baby," I said as we shook on it, "Ok now remember I'm the same one who told you, you was pregnant before you even knew," and laughed. "Mia Johnson, the doctor is ready for you," the nurse called. "Shorty, you got to change that last name before you have my babies," Semaj told me as we walked to the ultrasound room. I got undress and waited for the tech to come in, I looked over at Semaj and he was smiling, "I'm scared," I joked, but I really was nervous. The tech came in and begin to do the ultrasound as her and Semaj looked at the screen I heard them whispering and laughing, not long after she said, "Mia, you're having a girl..." I looked at Semaj and laughed, "I'll like my truck black to match.." before I could finish the tech said, " and baby b is a boy," Semaj jumped up, "I told you," as he lean over and gave me a kiss. I sat up and asked, "Let me see what you looking at," I couldn't believe it. I was already shocked I was having one baby now two. She printed out the pictures and sure enough there were two babies growing inside of me. As, I looked at the pictures while the doctor listen to their heartbeats I started to fall in love with the fact of being a mother and became full of joy.

We left the doctor and headed over to Semaj's parents house to tell them the news. I hadn't been over in a couple weeks so I was much bigger then the last time they saw me. "Pops where Ma at," Semaj asked as we walked in. Pops had retired from football so he was home more. "She's finishing up a call she'll be down in a minute." Pops said as he looked over at me, "Damn Mia, how many babies you carrying, five," We all laughed. The weight gain didn't really bother me because I was mostly all baby weight. "James leave Mia along she's still beautiful," Mrs. Davis said as she walked over and rubbed my stomach before sitting down. "So, what happen at the doctor," they asked. "Well Mia decided to bet me that if we have twins we would get married right after she graduate, but if it was one baby then I would have to buy her a Porsche Cayenne that she is in love with," Semaj told them, "Ok so who won the bet," Mrs. Davis asked. We both looked at each other and smiled, "He won," I said pulling the ultrasound pictures out handing them to them. "I knew it was more than one baby in there as big as you got in two weeks." Mr. Davis said as we all laugh. We sat a little before heading home, "Alright pops, I'm bout to spin I need to go feed my babies," Semaj said giving his dad five as I turned around screaming, "Semaj!!!" He looked at me and laugh, "Shorty, you almost six months pregnant you think they don't know we having sex." We all laughed as we went to the car to head home.

"Mia, we should go to Miami, before you have the twins to visit your O.G. and pops." Semaj and I were on the way home. We really didn't talk much about my life in Miami. I didn't like to talk about my past before. Now I really hated to talk about it afraid that Semaj would still want to seek revenge on my sick evil step-brothers. Semaj didn't talk about it because he always had plans to get revenge and knew that if I knew I would try and stop him. "Jay, I mean we have a lot going on." I hated to think of going to Miami, I had not been back to Miami since I moved to Chicago. I had no plans on going anytime soon either, "I am about to graduate, you just finish your first year of college we have to get prepare for not one baby but two now. We can go to Miami another time. Besides they will be coming up for my graduation, anyway." I was giving every excuse to not go to Miami. "Shorty, you haven't been to the crib for over five years, why you really don't want to go?" Semaj was pretty sure he knew the answer, and that's why he was going to take care of the situation for good. "Jay, what you want for dinner?" I figured it was time to change the subject.

As we pulled up to the condo, there was a familiar face standing in front of the building. "What you on, my G? I thought I told you not to come around here no more." Semaj jumped out the car. "Oh, I heard you was in town, and I needed to know, how the fuck you get this bitch pregnant, but made me have an abortion," Brittney stood in front of the building entrance, looking at me after saying that. "G, you wasn't never pregnant from me stop playing,"

Semaj said as I walked passed Brittney and into the building not even looking in her direction. "Jay, I'm not dealing with this tonight. She already flat my tires and try to bust the window out the car." Finally looking over at Brittney I continue, "you better thank God I am pregnant or else I would've been beat your ass." Semaj held the door for me to walk in. "So, you still treating her like she some type of Queen." Brittney looked at me with pure jealousy and hatred in her eyes, and I looked right back at her, "I'm his only Queen you remember that," I walked in the door and she was furious. "G, what you on, for real for real," Semaj asked before walking into the building. "She stole what was mine," Brittney yelled at the door. "You was never my shorty, and I was never yours," Semaj said as he walked in the door. We went into the house as we normally did and I started cooking dinner as Semaj sat on the sofa watching tv.

The phone rang, "Yo!" Semaj answered the phone. "Make sure you tell your girl I was the first one to carry your baby two different times" It was Brittney. "Man, you a goofy for real for real. How you get our number? You gone make me hurt you. Don't call our house no more!" Semaj slammed the phone down. "Shorty, I thought I told you to change the phone number, this mug tripping for real for real." Semaj walked in the kitchen. I set the food on the table so that we could eat dinner. "I forgot to change the number and she hadn't been calling so I figured she was done playing on the phone." I said as I sat down.

As we ate the phone ring at least ten times, but every time I would answer the person would just hang up. I let Semaj answer this time, "Merch, goofy you tweaking real hard stop playing on the phone my G!" Semaj was frustrated at this point. "Jay, this uncle Steve what you on, you good." Semaj laughed, "My bad Unk this goofy keep playing on the phone, chick mad cause Mia pregnant."

Uncle Steve didn't like the sound of that he knew a jealous woman was the most dangerous woman in the world. "Jay, be careful with that for real for real. She could be dangerous." Semaj didn't think it would get to the point that anyone would get hurt. "No, it won't get to that point, what's up Uncle Steve." Remembering the reason he called, "Yeah, but remember that conversation you had with Sherell?" Semaj had been trying to get information about my step-brothers since he found out what they had did to me without me finding out. Semaj got up from the table so that I couldn't hear, "Yeah, what about it?" "Well, I got Sherell to tell me a little more about the two dudes that violated Mia." Semaj walked to the door to make sure I was still at the table, "Word, what you know?" Semaj had been waiting for this information. "You don't need to know the details just know it's handled." Uncle Steve assured Semaj, but that wasn't good enough for him, "I want to be there when it's handled." I walked into the room, "When what's handled?" I scared Semaj.

I had learned a lot about Uncle Steve since meeting him. I knew he had people in almost every major city and was well respected and not to be played with. Some people considered him a dangerous man with the power to have people do whatever he wanted them to. "Shorty, don't worry about that it's nothing for you to worry about." Semaj kissed me on the forehead and quickly got off the phone with Uncle Steve. I let it go and figured it was nothing and got ready for bed.

I didn't get any sleep last night. Someone played on the phone the entire night, and every time I would answer the phone the person would just breathe on the phone not saying anything. I finally unplug the phone to get some rest. "Jay, Brittney played on the phone all night." As we got ready to leave I had school and Semaj was going to hang with his pops and uncles for the day. "I thought I heard the phone last night." Just as we were walking out the door the phone rang, and Semaj picked it up, "Yo!" "Hopefully your Queen doesn't fall down the stairs today, and hurt that precious baby of yours she's having" It was Brittney again. Semaj just hung up the phone, "Shorty this bitch tweaking hard." Semaj opened the door, and we left.

He decided to drive me to school after that last phone call. After dropping me off he went and met up with is dad and Uncle Steve as he had planned. He walked into the house, "Unk, what information you got for me," Semaj said as he sat down after embracing his dad and uncle. "Nephew, I already told you, it's handled." Uncle Steve said as he looked over at his twin brother. "Will you tell your son to let me handle this for him, so he could keep his hands clean." Semaj's dad looked over at him, "Jay, let Steve them handle this you got too much going on right now to focus on, plus you don't want to risk leaving Mia and the twins out here without you." Semaj just listen the last thing he would ever want is to not be there for Mia and his babies. Uncle Steve was excited, "Nephew, you didn't tell me yall was having twins. That means they was made through love, at least that's what your grandma always told us," they all laughed. They talked a little more and after some convincing Semaj agree that he would let Uncle Steve handle the situation, but they wasn't fully convinced he would.

Kim and I were walking together like always to go and wait for Semaj to come get us. "Mia, what's going on with Brittney. I heard the phone ringing all night long. I answered it and she said that she was pregnant by Semaj too." I looked at Kim in disbelief, "Kim does that even sound right?" Kim didn't even have to think about it, "I knew she was lying, but she has been calling my auntie and uncle telling them these lies." I couldn't believe this girl was doing the most. As they got ready to walk down the stairs, Brittney was standing right by the stairs smiling. "Speaking of the devil." we both said as we laughed and walked by her. "Be careful I wouldn't want you to fall," Brittney said as she walked off. I turned to face her, "Trust me the last thing I'm worried about is falling, or anything happening to me or my precious babies that I'm carrying." Brittney looked shocked. "Oh yeah, I heard your little threats this morning, now let me tell you something," I said walking back over to Brittney while Kim tried to pulled me back, "If you even think you going to do something to me or my babies you better think again, because you might think you crazy, but I'm crazier for real, now you want to try me." I said as I rubbed my big pregnant belly. Semaj pulled up right on time and jumped out the car, "Mia, what you doing?" He said as he pulled me back stepping in between Brittney and I. "So, she's good enough to have two babies, but I couldn't even have one of your kids. Even after I begged you to get me pregnant." Brittney scream running up to Semaj. "Mia, get in the car," Semaj turned around and I knew that look all too well, I grab his arm, "No we are both getting in the car" I pulled him as Brittney continue to yell, "I want my life back, that's my car you gave her, that's supposed to be my baby she's having. She's living my life." I looked at Brittney as Semaj walked to get back in the car. "Maybe, she is crazier than me," I said with a laugh. "Mia what the hell was you doing," Semaj said as he got in the car rubbing my stomach. "Jay, I wasn't about to fight, I'm not that crazy, but I'm not going to keep letting this chick threaten us." I said grabbing my stomach. "Well let Kim handle it next time," Semaj said looking back at Kim. "Jay I tried to stop her, but Mia is stronger than she looks especially when she's pressed." Kim try to plead her cased. "I know she's a firecracker, but I need you to make sure she doesn't do anything to harm herself or my babies for real for real." Semaj said as we rode down the street. "Why this chick keep saying she was pregnant and she's calling around telling ma and pops she's pregnant too," I was still pissed and this Brittany situation was becoming too much for me. "Mia, please calm down, you know this stress is not good for you and the babies," Semaj said trying to get me to calm down. "Semaj, was she ever pregnant from you and don't lie to me," I scream slapping his hand off of my stomach. "No, that bitch wasn't never pregnant from me, Mia stop with this shit for real for real," Semaj told me. "I'm not feeling good, just take me to Sherell house," I told Semaj as I picked up the phone to call Sherell. "Mia, you not going to no dam Sherell's house and if you caused this goofy to stress you and you hurt my babies…" Semaj said as I looked in the mirror and saw a car speeding up behind us, "Jay, do you see this car flying about to hit us." He looks in the rearview mirror and noticed it was Brittney's car. "She gone make me kill her for real for real," Semaj slammed on breaks jumping out the car. Brittney cut over in the next lane barely miss hitting us and as she passed she screamed, "It's not over!!"Kim warned me, "Mia you better be careful with her I've heard she comes from a dangerous family."

# SNATCHED IN
## COULDN'T LET GO

# *DON'T TAKE MY BABY*

Brittney was the product of a pimp and his bottom bitch. Her mom had been hoeing for a pimp by the name of Slick. Slick was married when Brittney was conceived. Brittney's mom Andrea, figure that now was her chance to get out the game and replace Slick's main lady since she had his only baby, but that wasn't what Slick had planned. He took Brittney from Andrea and gave her to his wife for them to raise as their own. Which left Andrea at the bottom of the bunch with the rest of the hoes he had. "Slick, I thought we were going to be together if I had your baby," Andrea pleaded with Slick as he packed Brittney up at only six weeks old. "Bitch, I only picked you to have the baby because you're my Spanish hoe. Now, go make me some more money and bring me some more hoes, than we can talk about you being my main bitch." Slick told Andrea as he pushed her into a room with three Johns that was waiting for her services only six weeks after giving birth to his child. "Ok daddy, but please don't take my baby. I'll do whatever you want me to, just don't take Brittney from me." Andrea begged Slick as he walked out with their baby.

"Slick, when you going let me see my baby? She needs to know her real momma." Andrea asked as he was taking her to another John. She had not seen her baby in 3 months. Every time she would ask about the baby Slick would give her the same response, "Bitch worry about my money, you don't make enough money for me, how you gone take care of a baby." He would always say right before putting her out the car to turn a trick. "I'm coming to get my baby tonight," Andrea told Slick before going to do her job. She wanted her baby, and she was going to get her by any means necessary. Anybody that tried to stop her was going to be dealt with them however she saw fit for them.

Later that night Andrea showed up to Slick's main house that he shared with his wife and knocked on the door. A small thick pretty brown skin lady opens the door holding a baby, which Andrea believe was her baby, Brittney. "Hi, may I help you?" The lady asked as Andrea stared at the baby. "Yeah, where Slick at?" Andrea tried to push her way inside the house as the lady blocked her. "Who are you and what are you doing at my house?" The lady tried to close the door as Andrea continue to push the door open. As she overpowers the lady holding the baby, she pushes the door open causing the lady to fall backwards. Andrea enters the house and pulls out a gun as she closes the door. "I just want my baby. I don't want to hurt nobody." Andrea told the lady as she pointed the gun at her. "You going to have to kill me if you think I'm just going to give you my baby." The lady tries to stand up and immediately was knocked back down as blood started to rush down her arm. "You shot me!" The lady screams as Slick walks in the door. "Bitch what are you doing at my house," Slick said as he looked over at his wife, noticing she was shot. He looked back at Andrea, "Did you shoot my wife?" Slick said walking toward Andrea. "It was an accident, daddy," Andrea was afraid of what Slick was going to do to her. She closed her eyes and pulled the trigger. Pow, Pow, Pow, when she opened her eyes she saw Slick laying on the floor with blood coming out his mouth, and chest. She ran over and grabbed her baby and got all the money that Slick had on him before running out the door.

She jumped in Slick's car and rode around for a little while until she could figure out where to go. She hadn't talked to her mom in over a year around the same time she met Slick. She pulled over in front of a house she used to call home. She grabs the baby who had no clue of what just took place and was peacefully sleeping, and walked to the front door. Before she could knock on the door, it swung open, and she was face to face with her mother. "Andrea!!!" Her mother screamed as she hugged her, "I've been waiting for this day to come and you've finally come home," Her mother told her as she pulled her in finally noticing the baby in the car seat sitting on the porch. "Andrea, who's baby?" Her mother asked still happy she was finally able to see her daughter again. "Mommy I need your help," Andrea said as she picked up the baby from the car seat. "I need you to watch over my baby for a little while. I just killed her dad and shot his wife," Andrea said in disbelief of what she had done. "What!!! Andrea, what do you mean…" her mom asked. "Listen, mommy they try to take my baby from me, and I had to get her back," Andrea said as she handed Brittney to her grandmother to meet for the first time. "Oh my goodness she's beautiful Andrea," her mother said as the baby opened her eyes and looked up at her.

Andrea's mother whose name is Maria took the baby

and bathed her. Afterwards, she cooked and told Andrea to take a shower and eat. After Andrea took her shower and ate, she jumped up and looked out the window realizing she still had Slick's car. "Mommy I have to go the police will be looking for me soon," Andrea said as she started to walk to the door she handed her mom over fifteen thousand dollars that she got off of Slick when she took Brittney. "Here mommy take this and take care of Brittney until I can get everything worked out." Andrea kissed her baby and walked out the door.

Andrea went into hiding and ditched Slick's car. She left Chicago that night, and she planned never to return. Slick had never said her name, and she had never seen his wife before tonight. So, she figured if she stayed away from Chicago and just maybe the wife would forget all about her. Andrea headed down south with one of Slick's other hoes and made her home in a little country town called Augusta, Georgia. She would call and check in on Brittney and send money weekly to make sure that her mom was able to take care of Brittney the way she wanted her taken care of.

It had been five years since Andrea had left Chicago and she had heard that Slicks wife had remarried and had another baby a year after Slick's death. Andrea knew that she needed to get her mom and daughter out of Chicago because Brittney was about to start school and she didn't want her daughter to end up in the same school as Slick's wife's child and risk her seeing Brittney. She took a chance and went back up to Chicago to try to convince her mom to leave Chicago. As she knocked on the door, she saw a little girl running from the backyard. She knew from the pictures that was Brittney. "Hello Brittney it's momma," Andrea said as Brittney walked up to her. "Hi momma I've been waiting for you," Brittney ran up and hugged her mom. They walked into the house and Maria was just as happy to see her daughter as she was when she last saw her five years ago. "Andrea, why didn't you tell me you were coming," Maria said as they sat down.

"Mommy, I want you and Brittney to leave Chicago," Andrea told her mom after she had put Brittney to sleep. Shaking her head, Maria said, "No Andrea, this is all we know I can't just leave Chicago our family is here. Why do you want us to move?" Maria asked. "Mommy, Slicks wife got remarried and had a baby a year after the incident happen with him, and now that Brittney's about to start school I don't want to risk the chance of her ever running into Brittney," Andrea tried to explain to her mom. "Listen, I'm not moving this child all over the world to cover up something you did," Maria told Andrea as she walked into the kitchen to clean up. "Mommy, what I did? I did what I had to do to get my baby back." Andrea said as she followed her mom into the kitchen, "Ok, mommy what about if I buy you a house on the Northside of Chicago would you move over there," Andrea offered her mom. "Yeah, I've always wanted to live on the Northside of town anyway, but Andrea how are you going to pay for this house," Maria asked which she normally never got into Andrea business and asked any question about the money she would send her to take care of Brittney. She just knew houses on the Northside you had to have money to live over there. "Mommy, you don't worry about that the house will be yours in your name so that nobody could ever take it from you if that's what you are worried about," Andrea assured her mom.

The next day the three of them went house shopping with Andrea's friend who had come up with her. After looking and looking for hours, Andrea finally found a house that she felt was perfect for her daughter to be raised in. "Mommy this is the one," Andrea said as they all stood in front of an all-white two-story home. "Andrea this is too big for us," Maria told her daughter. "Mommy nothings too big for my princess." Andrea looked at her friend, "This is the one." He nodded walking off and got on the phone. After standing there for about ten minutes, a lady drove up and open the house up for them to enter. "Who's name will the house be in," the woman asked as she pulled paperwork out and sat it on the table. "It's going to be in Maria Rivers name," Andrea said as she pointed at her mom. "Ma'am I just need you to sign here, here, and here before I can hand over the keys," she said pointing to the sections she needs to be signed. Maria looked over at Andrea as Andrea motion for her to go ahead, "Mommy the house was pay for in cash, so you don't have anything to worry about." Andrea told her mom right before she signed the papers.

Andrea moved her mom and daughter into their new home leaving everything in their old home. She furnishes and buys everything new. Including their clothes. Andrea didn't want them going back to their old house for anything. She made sure they had everything they needed and wanted, and the same way she came in she left without anyone ever knowing.

# In Disbelief

Brittney had been known to be the center of attention. She was very well known around the school, and not for being the good smart girl, but for being the easiest girl to get a kitty boost with. She was known to sleep with anybody she thought had money just to get them to buy her things. Her latest love interest just happens to be the most popular boy in the school, Semaj Davis, the son of the wide receiver James Davis. "Momma, he's not into me anymore. He's all up this bitch Mia's ass now," Brittney told her mom as she got dress for school. "Well what you going to do you gone let some hoe come in and take your man or you going to do something about it," Andrea asked Brittney. "I got a planned I'm going to get pregnant by him and I'll be set for life," Brittney told her mom as she got dress for school that morning. "That's right baby girl don't ever give no pussy to nobody who can't take care of you," her mom told her before hanging up the phone.

She went to school that day, and she saw Semaj chasing behind me as he had been doing for the past four years since I moved up from Miami. "Semaj, why you keep running behind her when you could have all this whenever you want it," Brittney said as she places his hand between her legs. "Yeah alright, I'm gone slide tonight then," Semaj told her pulling his hand back and walking off. She wanted a relationship with Semaj, and all he wanted was to hit it and keep it moving. That's the way it had been between them, and that's the way he wanted to keep it. His focus was trying to get me. Brittney was just right to have fun with for the moment.

That night as Brittney got dress for Semaj to come pick her up she had one thing on her mind, and that was to convince Semaj not to wear a condom. Semaj pulled up to Brittney's house, "Shorty, I love you for real for real," he told me as we got ready to hang up the phone. "Have a better night Jay," I said as I hung up the phone. Semaj blew the horn and Brittney ran out the door. "Hey baby, it took you long enough," Brittney said as she tried to kiss him. He pushed her back, "You know I don't kiss, you tweaking for real for real," Semaj said as he pulled off. "Semaj, I think we should start taking our relationship serious," Brittney said as they pulled up to West Belmont to City Suites Chicago. "What relationship you are tweaking you ain't my shorty. I poke, and you go home, you know that's what it is, don't try to catch feelings now. I'm coolin on that with you," Semaj said as he parked. "Why you always bring me to these hotels, I'm not good enough to take to your house," Brittney asked as she followed Semaj to the room. "Look G, what's up with you? Ain't shit change you no the rules if you, not my shorty you don't go to my house. And you, not my shorty," Semaj told Brittney as he opens the hotel room door. "I bet if I was that bitch, Mia, I could go to the house then," Brittney said as she followed him inside. "Watch your mouth, and you could never be Mia,"

Semaj said as he laughed, " Let's just do what we came to do," he said as he pushes Brittney's head between his legs. After giving him head Semaj went to put on a condom, and Brittney grabbed his hand, "You don't have to put that on I ain't been sleeping with nobody else. Plus, I want to feel you inside me. I never felt you raw," Semaj laughed as he put the condom on, "And you never will." Semaj was getting ready to drop Brittney off and decided that was the last time he was going to be involved with her. "Look G, we had a couple of great kitty boost, but after tonight I'm good. I can't be on that with you no more." As they pulled up to Brittney's house, she couldn't believe what he was saying, "Naw, you don't mean that. Mia could be your main girl I don't mind," Brittney didn't like the thought of Semaj, and his money was about to walk out of her life. "You tweaking for real for real," Semaj said as he handed Brittney three hundred dollars, "G, I got to spin he said as Brittney got out the car and he pulled off.

It was right before the pep rally and Kris had just embarrassed Brittney after she tried to step to me over Semaj. She overheard Tim saying he wanted to get at me and she figured she would give him some juice on her and Semaj's relationship or should I say the lack of relationship. "Tim, so you like that bitch too," Brittney said as Semaj was running off. "G, you tweaking Mia decent for real for real," Tim told Brittney as they started to walk. " Well, why don't you tell her that me and Semaj still messing around. I'm sure that will open the door for you. She'll never want Semaj after she finds out he's poking someone else especially me," Brittney told Tim and walked off.

After the game, Brittney figured she'll try to get Semaj to come pick her up again tonight and try to put a hole in the condom this time. "So you gone slide tonight," Brittney cut Semaj off as he was walking out the locker room. "G, I told you last night I'm not on that with you no more," Semaj told Brittney as they both looked up and saw me headed their way. "Dam," Semaj said, "Man don't say nothing to her, she liable to pop off on you tonight for real for real," Semaj warned Brittney. "Hey, let me get the keys to the car it's cold out here." I held my hand out as Semaj looked for his keys. "Girl, he doesn't let nobody hold the keys to his…." Before Brittney could finish, Semaj handed me the keys. I looked at Brittney smiled and walked off, "Don't take too long Jay. Handle your business playboy" I never looked back.

Brittney was going through all the times she had tried to get Semaj to forget about me and just be with her as she speeds down the street after almost running into us. "How could he give her my life, how is she the one pregnant. Hell, I even offered to be the other woman, and he told me no! What's so good about her?" Brittney screamed to herself…….

# *Snatched In*
## *COULDN'T LET GO*

# *Coming Soon*

Made in the USA
Columbia, SC
31 May 2018